PETER CAMENZIND

Peter Camenzind

HERMANN HESSE

TRANSLATED BY MICHAEL ROLOFF

Picador
Farrar, Straus and Giroux
New York

www.picadorusa.com

Picador® is a U.S. registered trademark and is used by Farrar, Straus and Giroux under license from Pan Books Limited.

For information on Picador Reading Group Guides, as well as ordering, please contact the Trade Marketing department at St. Martin's Press.
Phone: 1-800-221-7945 extension 763
Fax: 212-677-7456
E-mail: trademarketing@stmartins.com

ISBN 0-312-42263-6 ISBN: 978-0-312-42263-9

First published in the United States by Farrar, Straus and Giroux

First Picador Edition: December 2003

P1

PETER CAMENZIND

Chapter One

IN THE BEGINNING was the myth. God, in his search for self-expression, invested the souls of Hindus, Greeks, and Germans with poetic shapes and continues to invest each child's soul with poetry every day.

As a child I knew no names for the lake, mountains, and brooks where I grew up. My eyes beheld the broad, smooth, þlue-green lake lying in the sun, glistening with tiny lights and wreathed by precipitous mountains whose highest crevices were filled with glazed snow and thin waterfalls, and at whose feet there sloped luminous meadows with orchards and huts and gray Alpine cattle. And on my poor little soul, still blank and calm and full of expectancy, the lake and mountain spirits etched their proud deeds. Rigid cliffs and scarred precipices spoke, in tones of awe and defiance, of the age that had given them birth. They spoke of ancient days when the earth heaved and tossed and, in the moaning agony of birth, thrust mountain peaks and crests from its tortured womb. Rock masses surged upward, screaming and cracking until, aiming into nowhere, they toppled. Twin mountains wrestled desperately for space until one rose triumphant, pushing his brother aside and smashing him. Even today you can find broken-off crags, toppled or split, clinging precariously to the edge of a gorge. During each thaw, torrents sweep down blocks of rock the size of houses, shattering them like glass or implanting them in the soft meadows.

These mountains proclaim a message that is easy to understand when you have seen their steep walls and layers upon layers of rock, twisted, cracked, filled with gaping wounds. "We have suffered most brutally," they announce, "and we are suffering still." But they say it proudly, sternly, and with clenched teeth, like ancient, indomitable warriors.

Yes, warriors. I saw them do battle with lake and storm in the harrowing nights of early spring, when the angry Föhn raged about their hoary peaks and the torrents tore raw pieces from their flanks. They stood there at night—breathless and unyielding, their roots stubbornly straddling the ground, exposing cleft, weather-beaten walls and crags to the storm, gathering their strength as they crowded together defiantly. With each fresh wound they received, I heard their dreadful roar of rage and fear; their terrible moans resounded through the remotest valleys, broken and angry.

And I beheld meadows and slopes and earth-filled crevices covered with grass, flowers, ferns, and mosses that bore odd and ominous old provincial names. These were the children and grandchildren of the mountains and led colorful, harmless lives. I touched and examined them, smelled their perfumes and learned their names. It was the sight of the trees, however, that affected me most deeply. I saw each tree leading a life of its own, formed in its own particular shape, casting its own individual shadow. Being recluses and warriors, they seemed to have greater kinship with the mountains, for each tree—especially those in the upper reaches—had to struggle tenaciously against wind, weather, and rock to survive and grow. Each had to bear its own burden and cling desperately, thereby acquiring its own shape and wounds. There were Scotch pines with branches extending only on one side, and some whose red trunks crawled snakelike around protruding rocks so that trees and rocks pressed and clung together in a tight embrace, preserving each other. These trees gazed at me like warriors and inspired respect and awe in my heart.

Our men and women resembled these trees. They were hard, stern, and close-lipped—the best of them the most so. Thus I learned to look on men as trees and rocks, and to honor and love them as I did the quiet pines.

Nimikon, our hamlet, is situated on a triangular slope hemmed in on two sides by protrusions of rock, on the other by the lake. One path leads to the nearby monastery, the second to a neighboring village four and a half hours away by foot. Other villages bordering the lake can be reached only by boat. Our cottages, built of timber frame in the old style, are of no discernible age. A new cottage is rarely built; old buildings are repaired piecemeal, as required—one year the floor, the next a section of the roof. Many half beams and boards, once part of the living-room wall, and still too good to be used as firewood, come in handy when the stable or barn needs repair or the front door a new crosspiece. The people who live in these cottages undergo similar transformations: each of them plays his part as long as he can, then withdraws reluctantly into the circle of extreme old age, finally sinking into oblivion—not that much fuss is made about it. If you returned after many years' absence, you would find everything unchanged— a few old roofs renewed and a few new ones grown old. The old men you knew would have disappeared, to be sure, but only to be replaced by other old men who inhabit the same cottages, bear the same names, watch over the same dark-haired brood of children whose faces and gestures are scarcely distinguishable from those they have succeeded.

What our community lacked was a frequent infusion of fresh blood and life. Almost all the inhabitants, a passably vigorous breed, are the closest of cousins; at least three-quarters of them are called Camenzind. This name fills the pages of the church register and can be found on most of the crosses in the graveyard. It is crudely engraved or painted in loud colors on houses, wagoner's carts, stable buckets, and lake boats. My father's house bears the following painted legend: *This house hath been built by Jost and Francisca Camenzind,* referring not to my father but to his predecessor, my great-grandfather. When I die, even if childless, I can be sure that another Camenzind will settle in the old house, provided it is still standing and has a roof.

Despite this surface uniformity, our small hamlet had in it good people and bad, eminent and lowly, powerful and impotent. Side by side with a number of clever ones, there flourished an amusing handful of fools—not counting the village idiots, that is. Here, as elsewhere, the large world was represented in small, and since the mighty and the lowly, the sly and the foolish were inextricably related and intermarried, it was no surprise to find overweening pride and narrow-minded silliness jostling each other under the same roof—our life had sufficient breadth and scope for the entire range of human life. Yet a permanent veil of suppressed or subliminal uneasiness hung over all of us. The wretchedness of a life of unrelieved toil and dependence on the forces of nature had in the course of time invested our declining race with a penchant for melancholy. Though this may have suited our rough, angular faces, it failed to produce fruit—at least any that afforded pleasure. For that reason we were glad to have in our midst a sprinkling of fools, who, though only comparatively foolish, provided a touch of color and some occasion for laughter and mockery. Whenever an incident or escapade made one of them the butt of local gossip, merriment would flash over the wrinkled, deeply tanned faces of the people of Nimikon, and the enjoyment of one's own superiority added a delicate philistine piquancy to the joke. They delightedly smacked their lips, feeling confident that they themselves were immune to such aberrations and gaffes. To this majority—who occupied a middle ground between the righteous and the sinners, and gladly would have accepted the honors accorded both—my father belonged. Every piece of tomfoolery filled him with blissful uneasiness: he would teeter back and forth between genuine admiration of the culprit and smug awareness of his own innocence.

One of these fools was my Uncle Konrad. Not that he was less bright than my father or any other villager. Quite the contrary. He was sly enough, driven by an ambitious spirit that the others might well have envied. Yet nothing went right for him. To his credit, he did not hang his head or become despondent over his failures; instead, he renewed his efforts and even displayed a remarkable awareness of the tragi-comical aspect of all his endeavors. However, this last trait was ascribed to comic eccentricity and merely earned him a place among the community's unpaid jesters. My father's attitude toward Uncle Konrad was a constant tug-of-war between admiration and contempt. Each new project of his filled my father with avid curiosity and excitement, which he sought to hide behind deceptively ironic inquiries and allusions. He would restrain himself until Uncle Konrad, certain of success, began putting on airs, whereupon my father joined the genius in fraternal speculation. When the inevitable catastrophe followed, my uncle would shrug it off, while my father heaped fury and insults on him and then would not favor him with a single word or glance for months.

It is to Uncle Konrad that our village is indebted for its first sight of a sailboat, an experiment in which my father's skiff was a partial sacrifice. My uncle had copied the sail and rigging from calendar woodcuts, and could hardly be blamed if our skiff lacked the necessary beam to carry a sail. The preparations took weeks, with my father on tenterhooks from all the tension, hope, and anxiety, while the rest of the village talked of little else than Konrad Camenzind's new venture. It was a memorable event when the boat was finally launched on a windy day in late summer. My father, filled with forebodings of imminent disaster, did not attend the launching and, to my great disappointment, had forbidden me to go along. Baker Füssli's son was the sailing expert's sole companion. The entire village assembled on our graveled patch and in our little garden to witness the extraordinary spectacle. A snappy off-shore wind was blowing, but the baker's son had to row until the breeze caught the sail and it bellied out; then the boat skimmed proudly away. Admiringly, we watched them disappear around the nearest mountain spur and prepared to accord my clever uncle a victor's welcome; we resolved to feel properly ashamed for all snide doubts we had previously entertained. The boat returned that night—without its sail, the sailors more dead than alive. The baker's son coughed and sputtered: "You missed the best part, you almost had yourselves a double funeral next Sunday." My father had to replace two planks in the skiff and since that day no sail has been reflected in our lake's blue surface. For a long time afterwards, whenever my uncle was in a hurry, people would shout at him: "Use your sails, Konrad!" Father bottled up his anger and for a long while would avert his eyes when he encountered his unlucky brother-in-law; spittle squirted in a wide arc as a sign of his unspeakable contempt. This state of affairs prevailed until Konrad approached him with his project for a fireproof oven, a scheme which brought infinite ridicule down on its inventor's head and ended up costing my father four whole talers. Woe to anyone who dared remind him of the four-taler episode! Much later, when our household was again in financial straits, my mother casually remarked how nice it would be if the criminally wasted money were available now. My father turned purple but controlled himself; he merely said: "I wish I'd drunk it all up some Sunday."

Toward the end of each winter the Föhn approached with a roar. The terrified people of the Alps listened to it, trembling; yet, when away from home, they always long to hear it.

The Föhn's approach could be sensed by men and women, bird and beast and mountain, several hours beforehand. Its actual arrival, heralded almost always by cool counter-winds, announced itself with a deep whirring. The blue-green lake instantly turned ink-black and was suddenly covered with scudding white-caps. Though inaudible only minutes before, it soon thundered against the shore like an angry sea. At the same time the entire landscape seemed to huddle to-gether. You could now discern individual rocks on pin-nacles that usually brooded in remote heights, and could distinguish roofs, gables, and windows in villages that heretofore lay like brown dots in the distance. Everything appeared to close in—mountains, meadows, houses, like a frightened herd. Then the grumbling roar began; the ground trembled. Whipped-up waves were driven through wide stretches of air as spume, and the

(9

desperate struggle between storm and mountain rang
continually in one's ears, especially at night. A little
later, news would spread through the villages of choked
mountain brooks, smashed houses, wrecked skiffs,
missing fathers and sons.

As a child, I was afraid of the Föhn, even hated it.
But with the awakening of boyhood wildness, I was
glad to welcome this insurgent, eternally youthful, inso-
lent harbinger of spring. It was marvelous as the Föhn
embarked on its ferocious struggle, full of life and
exuberance, storming, laughing, groaning, bending the
rough old pines with brutal hands so that they moaned.
Later my love of the Föhn deepened as I welcomed it
for bringing the beauty of the sweet, superbly rich
south, from which emanated streams of joy, warmth,
and beauty that were hurled against the mountains in
our flat, cool northlands. Nothing could be stranger or
more delicious than the sweet Föhn fever that overcomes the people in the mountain regions, especially
the women, whom it robs of sleep, tantalizing their
senses. It is the south, hurling itself with all its heat
and violence against the breast of the coarser, poorer
north, informing the snowed-in Alpine villages that the
primrose, the narcissus, and the almond trees are in
flower again on the shores of Italian lakes.

Once the Föhn subsided and the last grimy avalanches melted, the most beautiful season began. Then

yellowish meadows blossomed mountainward on all sides; snow-capped peaks and glaciers led a contented existence in their pure reaches; the lake turned warm blue and mirrored the sun, the procession of clouds.

All this was certainly enough to round out childhood, and even a lifetime. For all these events spoke the loud and unbroken language of God, which never crossed the lips of man. If you have heard God's words proclaimed in this fashion during childhood, you will be able to hear them echo within you for the rest of your days, sweet, strong, terrible; you will never escape their spell. A native of the mountains can study philosophy and natural history, and even dispense with God altogether, but when he experiences the Föhn or hears an avalanche crash through the forest, his heart trembles and he thinks of God and death.

My father's cottage had a tiny, fenced-in garden where bitter lettuce, beets, and cabbage grew and where my mother had laid out a touchingly narrow, barely sufficient flower bed: two China rose bushes, dahlia, and a handful of mignonette languished hopefully but miserably. The garden bordered an even narrower graveled area that reached as far as the lake. There stood two defunct barrels, a few planks and some fence posts to which we moored our boat, which at that time was still patched and caulked every few years. The days on which this operation was carried out are affixed in

my memory: warm afternoons in early summer, butterflies tumbling over the little garden in the sunlight,
the lake as smooth as oil, blue and still and softly irides-
cent, the mountain peaks thinly veiled in mist; the
gravel nearby smelling strongly of pitch and oil paint.
The boat would smell of tar all summer, and whenever
in later life I came upon the peculiarly distinctive odor
of tar and water I instantly visualized our graveled
landing area, with my father, in shirtsleeves, plying the
paint brush, bluish smoke curling from his pipe into the
summer air, brilliant sulphur butterflies unsteadily performing their hesitating flights. On those days my
father was always in a high good humor: he whistled
(which he could do superbly) and he might even give
forth with one brief yodel—this, however, mezzo-forte.
Then my mother would cook something good for
dinner. I now think she did it in the secret hope that
Camenzind would not go off to the tavern that evening.
But he went all the same.

I cannot claim that when I was young my parents
either noticeably hampered or furthered my mental
development. Mother always had her hands full of
work, and nothing in the world interested my father
less than questions of child-rearing. He had plenty to do
tending his few fruit trees, cultivating the little potato
patch, and seeing to his crop of hay. But every few
weeks, on the way home in the evening, he would take

me by the hand and proceed to the hayloft without a word. There a strange rite of chastisement and atonement was enacted: I was given a thrashing, and neither my father nor I ever quite knew why. These were mute sacrifices at the altar of Nemesis, offered up as a guilty tribute to an ineffable power, without scolding on his part or crying on mine. Any mention of "blind fate" later in my life reminded me of these mystic scenes; they seemed to me a graphic representation of this concept. Unknowingly, my father was obeying a simple pedagogic precept that life practices on all of us when it lets lightning strike, leaving us to ponder what misdeeds provoked the powers above. Unfortunately, such reflection rarely if ever occupied me; for the most part I accepted each installment of punishment passively, perhaps even stubbornly, always without the desirable self-examination and always glad, on those evenings, that once again I had done my share, that I had a few weeks' respite ahead of me. I was far less passive, however, when it came to my father's efforts to get me to work. Incomprehensible, bountiful nature had combined within me two diametrically opposed talents: unusual physical strength and an equally strong disinclination to work. My father exerted every effort to make a useful son and helper out of me, and I resorted to every possible ruse to evade the tasks imposed; no hero of antiquity, when I attended school, commanded my sympathy more than Hercules, who was compelled to perform those renowned, irksome labors.

I knew of nothing more wonderful than roaming idly about the mountains and meadows or along the lake. Mountains, lake, storm, and sun were my companions. They told me stories, molded me, and were dearer to me for many years than any person or any person's fate. But what I loved above all else, even more than the glistening lake, the mournful pines, and the sunny rocks, were the clouds.

Show me a man anywhere in the whole wide world who knows and loves clouds more than I! Or show me anything more beautiful. They are a plaything and comfort to the eye, a blessing and a gift of God; they also contain wrath and the power of death. They are as delicate, soft, and gentle as the souls of newborn babes, as beautiful, rich, and prodigal as good angels, yet somber, inescapable, and merciless as the emissaries of death. They hover as a silvery film, and sail past smiling and gold-edged; they hang poised, tinged yellow, red, and blue. Darkly, slowly they slink past like murderers, roaring head-over-heels like mad horsemen, drooping sadly and dreamily in the pale heights like melancholy hermits. They assume the shapes of blessed isles and guardian angels, resemble threatening hands, fluttering sails, migrating cranes. They hover between God's heaven and the poor earth like beautiful likenesses of man's every yearning and partake of both realms—dreams of the earth in which the sullied soul cleaves to the pure heaven above. They are the eternal symbol of all voyaging, of every quest and yearning for home. And as the clouds are suspended faintheartedly and longingly and stubbornly between heaven and earth, the souls of men are suspended faintheartedly and longingly and stubbornly between time and eternity.

O lovely, floating, restless clouds! I was an ignorant child and loved them, watched them, little knowing that I would drift through life like a cloud—voyaging, everywhere a stranger, hovering between time and eternity. Ever since childhood they have been my dear friends and sisters. There is not a street I cross without our nodding and greeting each other. Nor did I ever forget what they taught me then: their shapes, their features, their games, their roundelays and dances, their repose, and their strange stories in which elements of heaven and earth mingled.

Particularly the tale of the Snow Princess, which has the middle mountain ranges for a setting, early in winter, as warm air flows in from the lower reaches. The Snow Princess, coming down from immense heights, appears on this stage in the company of a small retinue and looks for a place of repose in the broad mountain hollows or on a summit. The false

North Wind enviously watches the trusting maiden lie down to rest and inches voraciously up the mountain, to fall upon her suddenly with a furious roar, tossing black-cloud rags at the beautiful Princess, mocking her, intent on chasing her away. Momentarily the Princess is disconcerted, but she waits and patiently suffers her adversary; sometimes she retreats unhappily, in quiet scorn, to her former height. At other times she gathers her frightened entourage about her, unveils her dazzlingly regal countenance, and motions the ogre to stand back. He temporizes, howls, then flees. And she beds down quietly and shrouds her throne in white mists as far as the eye can see. When the mist has withdrawn, the peaks and hollows lie clear, glistening with pure soft new snow.

This story has something in it so noble, of such soulfulness, has in it so much of beauty's triumph that I was enthralled by it; my heart stirred as with a happy secret.

Soon the time came when I was allowed to approach the clouds, walk among them, and gaze down upon their host from above. I was ten years old when I climbed my first mountain, the Sennalpstock, at whose foot lies our hamlet, Nimikon. That was the first time I beheld both the terror and beauty of the mountains. Gaping ravines, filled with ice and half-melted snow, glass-green glaciers, moraines ugly beyond belief, and suspended above all this, like a bell, the dome of heaven. When you have lived for ten years surrounded by mountains and hemmed in between mountain and lake, you can never forget the day you see your first wide sky above you, and the first boundless horizon. Even on the ascent I was amazed at how huge the familiar crags and cliffs really were. And now, quite overcome, I saw with fear and joy in my heart the immense distances bearing down upon me. So that was how fabulously wide the world was! And our village, lost in the depth below, was merely a tiny, light-colored speck. Pinnacles that had seemed to be within walking distance lay days apart.

I guessed that I had had only a glimpse of the world, not a full view at all. I realized that mountains could rise and crumble out there in the world, and great events transpire, without the slightest whisper reaching our isolated hamlet. Yet something quivered within me, like a compass needle striving with great energy, unconsciously, toward those great distances. And as I gazed into the infinite distances into which the clouds were voyaging, I grasped something of their beauty and melancholy.

My two adult companions praised my climbing as we rested briefly on the ice-cold summit. They were amused by my enthusiasm. Once recovered from my initial astonishment, I bellowed like a bull with joy and excitement, into the clear mountain air. This was my first inarticulate hymn to beauty. I expected a loud echo, but my voice died away in the peaceful heights like the faint cry of a bird. Then I felt abashed and was silent.

That day was the beginning. One momentous event now succeeded another. For one thing, the men took me along on mountaineering trips more often, even on the more difficult climbs, and with a strange and uneasy ecstasy I penetrated the great secret of the heights. Then I was made village goatherd. On one of the slopes where I usually drove my beasts was a sheltered nook overgrown with cobalt-blue gentians and bright-red saxifrage. In all the world this was my favorite spot. I could not see the village from there, and only a narrow, gleaming strip of lake was visible across the rocks, but the flowers glowed in fresh, laughing colors, the blue sky hung like a canopy over needle-sharp peaks, and the tinkling goat bells mingled with the incessant roar of a nearby waterfall. There I sprawled in the warmth, gazed in wonderment at the hurrying white cloudlets, and yodeled softly to myself until the goats noticed my laxness and took advantage of it, indulging in all sorts of forbidden games and tricks. This idyllic existence suffered a rude interruption during the first weeks, when I fell into a gully with a goat that had strayed from the flock. The goat died, my head ached, and I received an unmerciful hiding. I ran away from home, and was recaptured amid curses and lamentations.

These adventures might well have been my first and last. In which case this little book would not have seen the light of day and quite a number of other efforts and foolish acts would not have been perpetrated. Presumably I would have married one of my cousins and might even lie frozen in some glacier now. That would not have been the end of the world either. However, everything turned out differently and it would be presumptuous to compare what happened with what might have been.

Occasionally my father would do a little work for the monastery in Welsdorf. One day he fell ill and ordered me to notify the monastery that he was unable to come. Instead of traipsing to the monastery myself, I borrowed pen and paper from a neighbor, wrote a courteous letter to the friars, handed it to the woman who regularly took messages there, and set off into the mountains on my own.

The following week I came home to find a priest sitting there, waiting for the person who had written the letter. I was afraid, but then the priest praised me and tried to persuade my father to let me become a student. Uncle Konrad was in good graces at the time and was consulted. He was inflamed by the idea that I should study and eventually attend the university and become a scholar and a gentleman. My father allowed himself to be convinced, and thus my future took its place alongside my uncle's other risky ventures—the fireproof oven, the sailboat, and his similarly fantastic schemes.

I entered then upon a period of intense study, especially in Latin, Biblical history, botany, and geography. At that time I thoroughly enjoyed my studies; it never occurred to me that I might be buying all this foreign matter at the cost of my home and many years of happiness. Nor was Latin solely to blame. My father would have liked to make a farmer of me even if I had known all the *viri illustres* by heart. But the shrewd man penetrated to my innermost being and discovered there, as its center of gravity, my cardinal virtue: lassitude. I dodged work whenever possible and would run off to the mountains or the lake or lie hidden on a slope, reading and dreaming and lazing away the time. Realizing this, my father finally gave up on me.

This then is a good moment to say a few words about my parents. My mother, who had been beautiful, retained only her firm, straight frame and lively, dark eyes. She was tall, vigorous, industrious, and quiet. Though she was certainly as intelligent as my father, and stronger, she did not rule the house, leaving the reins in his hands. He was of average height, with thin, almost delicate limbs, and a stubborn, sly head, a light-complexioned face lined with tiny, exceptionally expressive wrinkles. His forehead was marked by a deep vertical fold that darkened whenever he moved his brows, lending him a doleful, ailing expression. At those times he looked as if he were trying to recollect something very important but lacked all hope of ever finding out what it was. You could detect a certain strain of melancholy in him, but no one paid this any heed. For almost all people in our region were victims of a slightly dour turn of mind, caused by the long winters, the dangers, the harsh and wearying struggle for survival, and the isolation from the world outside.

I have inherited important traits from both my parents. A modest worldly wisdom, a trust in God, and a calm, taciturn disposition from my mother, and from my father, irresoluteness, the inability to handle money, and the art of drinking heavily and with full awareness of it. However, the last-mentioned trait was not in evidence during my tender years. I have my father's eyes and mouth, my mother's slow, heavy gait, her build and her strength. My father in particular, and our people in general, endowed me with natural peasant cunning but also with their melancholy and tendency to baseless fits of depression. Since it was my destiny for many years to make my way far from home, among strangers, I would have been better equipped had I taken a good measure of lightheartedness with me on my travels.

Fitted out with these characteristics and a new set of

clothes, I began my journey into life. My parents' gifts have stood me in good stead, for I went out into life and have held my own ever since. Yet something must have been amiss that science and a wordly life never set right. Though I can scale a mountain, row for more than ten hours at a stretch, and if necessary kill a man singlehanded even today, I am as incompetent as ever in the art of living. My early, one-sided preoccupation with the earth, flowers, and animals has stunted in me the growth of most social graces. Even today my dreams offer remarkable proof of how much I tend toward a purely animal existence. For I often dream of myself lying on some shore as an animal, generally as a seal, conscious of such an intense feeling of well-being that, on waking, the recovery of my human dignity fills me not with pride or joy but with regret.

I was given the usual preparatory-school education, although my board and tuition fees were waived; it was decided that I should become a philologist. No one knows exactly why. There isn't a more useless or more tiresome subject, and none with which I felt less kinship.

My school years passed quickly. Fights and lessons alternated with hours during which I felt homesick, and hours filled with impudent dreams about the future or devoted to the worship of science. In the midst of this, my innate lassitude would suddenly assert itself, getting me into all kinds of trouble, until thwarted by some new enthusiasm.

"Peter Camenzind," said my Greek professor, "you are stubborn and single-minded and one of these days you'll break your neck." I took a close look at the stout, bespectacled figure, calmly listened to his pronouncement, and found him amusing.

"Peter Camenzind," remarked the mathematics instructor, "you're a genius when it comes to wasting time and I regret that the lowest mark I can give you is zero. I estimate that your exercise today deserves a minus two and a half." I looked at him, pitied him because he squinted, and thought him very tedious.

"Peter Camenzind," my history professor once said, "you're no great shakes as a student, but you'll make a good historian all the same. You are lazy but you know how to differentiate between the momentous and the trivial."

Even that did not strike me as exceptionally important. Still, I respected my teachers because I thought they were in possession of the secret of science and science overawed me. And though my teachers were of one mind about my laziness, I managed to make some headway and my place in the classroom was just forward of center. Indeed, it did not escape me that school and school science were an inadequate patchwork, but I was biding my time. Beyond these preparations and fumblings there lay, I assumed, a realm of pure intellect and an unambiguous dead-certain science of truth. Once I reached this realm I would discover the meaning of the dark confusion of history, the wars of the nations, and the fearful questions that bother each and every soul.

Another yearning, however, held an even stronger and more urgent sway over me: I longed to have a friend. There was Kaspar Hauri, a brown-haired, serious-minded boy two years older than I, who had about him a calm and self-assured air, who held his head erect and spoke little to his classmates. I venerated him for months. I followed him about in the streets and longed to be noticed by him. I felt envious of every person he greeted and of every house I saw him leave or enter. But he was two classes ahead of me and presumably felt superior even to those in the same grade as he. We never exchanged as much as a single word. Instead, a puny, sickly boy attached himself to me, without any encouragement on my part. He was younger than I, timid and untalented, but he had beautiful doleful eyes and features. Because he was weak and somewhat misshapen, he was subjected to much bullying in his class and looked to me, strong and respected as I was, for protection. Soon he became too ill to attend school. I did not miss him and quickly forgot him altogether.

One classmate of mine was a boisterous fellow, short, fair-haired, and easygoing, with a thousand tricks up his sleeve—a musician, a mimic, and a clown. It took some doing on my part to win his friendship and this wily and irrepressibly cheerful little contemporary always treated me somewhat patronizingly. But at least I now had a friend. I visited him in his room, read a number of books with him, did his Greek homework, and in turn let him help me with math. We also went on a number of walks together and must have looked like bear and weasel on those occasions. He always dominated the conversation, was gay, witty, and completely at ease; I listened and laughed and was glad to have such a lighthearted friend.

One afternoon, however, I came upon him just as the little charlatan was amusing several friends with one of his favorite stunts. He had just impersonated one of the teachers when he called out: "Guess who this is!" And he proceeded to read a few lines from Homer, imitating my embarrassed demeanor, my nervous voice, my rasping country accent, and my habit of blinking and shutting my left eye when concentrating. It looked very funny and was rendered wittily and ruthlessly.

As he closed the book and collected his well-deserved applause, I stepped up to him from behind and had my revenge. I said nothing but gave my shame and wrath graphic expression with a single powerful slap in his face. Immediately afterwards the lesson began, and the teacher noticed my former friend's tears and his swollen red cheek—this boy was also his favorite pupil.

"Who did that to you?"

"Camenzind."

"Camenzind, stand up. Is that true?"

"Yes, sir."

"Why did you slap him?"

No reply.

"Did you have a reason?"

"No, sir."

So I was severely flogged and wallowed stoically in the ecstasy of innocent martyrdom. But since I was neither stoic nor saint but a schoolboy, I stuck my tongue out at my enemy after I had been punished—to its full length.

Horrified, the teacher let fly at me. "Aren't you ashamed of yourself? What is the meaning of this?"

"It's supposed to mean that he's a rat and I despise him. And he's a coward besides."

Thus ended my friendship with the mimic. He was to have no successor, and I was forced to spend my adolescence without a friend. And though my opinion of life and of mankind has undergone a number of changes since that time, I always remember that slap in the face with deep satisfaction, and I only hope the fair-haired boy hasn't forgotten either.

CHAPTER ONE

At seventeen I fell in love with a lawyer's daughter. She was beautiful and I am genuinely proud that all my life I have fallen in love only with very beautiful women. What I suffered because of her and other women, I will tell another time. Her name was Rösi Girtanner and even today she is worthy of the love of better men than I.

At that time, all the untapped vigor of youth coursed through my limbs. With my schoolmates I was forever becoming involved in the wildest scrapes. I was proud of being the best wrestler, batter, runner, and oarsman—yet I still felt melancholy. This had hardly anything to do with being unhappily in love. It was simply that sweet melancholy of early spring, which affected me more strongly than others, so that I derived pleasure from mournful visions of death and pessimistic notions. Of course, someone was bound to make me a gift of Heine's *Book of Songs*, in a cheap edition. What I did with this book did not really qualify as reading. I poured my overflowing heart into the empty verses, suffered with the poet, composed poems with him, and entered states of lyrical intoxication that were as well-suited to me as a nightgown to a little pig. Until that time I had had no idea of "literature." Now there followed in rapid succession Lenau, Schiller, Goethe, and Shakespeare; suddenly the pale phantom, literature, had become a god.

With a delicious shudder, I felt streaming toward me
from these books the cool but pungent fragrance of a
life not of this world yet real nonetheless, a life whose
waves now pounded where it sought to realize its fate—
in my ecstatic heart. In my reading nook in the attic
the only sounds to reach me were the hourly chimes
from the nearby tower and the dry clapping of nesting
storks, but there the characters of Shakespeare's and
Goethe's worlds walked in and out. The sublime and the
laughable aspects of everything human were revealed
to me: I realized the enigma of the sundered unruly
heart, the deep meaningfulness of the world's history,
and the mighty miracle of the spirit that transfigures
our brief stay and through the power of reason raises
our petty lives into the realm of fate and eternity. When
I stuck my head out through the narrow dormer window, I could see the sun shining on the roofs and
in the narrow alley. With astonishment I would listen
to the tangled small noises of work and everyday
existence rushing up. I sensed the loneliness and mys-
teriousness of my attic nook filling with great spirits as
in remarkably beautiful fairy tales. And gradually, the
more I read and the more strangely the roofs, streets,
and everyday life affected me, the more often I was
overcome by the timid and intimidating feeling that I
too might be a visionary: the world spread out before
me expected me to discover part of the treasure, to rip

the veil that covered the accidental and the common, to tear my findings out of chaos and immortalize them through the gift of poetry.

With some embarrassment I began composing a few poems, and gradually several notebooks filled up with verses, sketches, and short stories. They have perished; probably they were worth little, but they made my heart beat faster and filled me with ecstasy. My critical faculties and powers of self-examination were slow in catching up with these attempts. I did not experience my first great and necessary disappointment until my last year in school. I had already begun the destruction of my juvenilia—my scribbling had become suspicious to me—when I came upon a few volumes of Gottfried Keller's works, which I immediately read two or three times in succession. Then suddenly I realized how far removed my stillborn pipe dreams were from real, genuine, austere art. I burned my poems and stories, and with some of the embarrassed feeling that accompanies a hangover, I looked soberly and sadly out at the world.

Chapter Two

A S FOR LOVE, I must confess to having retained a youthful attitude to it all my life. For me, the love of women has been a purifying act of adoration, a flame shooting straight up from my melancholy, my hands stretched in prayer toward the blue heavens. Owing to my mother's influence and my own indistinct premonitions, I venerated womankind as an alien race, beautiful and enigmatic, superior to men by virtue of inborn beauty and constancy of character, a race which we must hold sacred. For, like stars and blue mountain heights, they are remote from us men and appear to be nearer to God. Since life did not always treat me gently, the love of women has been as bitter for me as it has been sweet. Although I still cherish women, my chosen role of solemn priest has often changed all too quickly into the painfully comic one of fool.

Rösi Girtanner and I passed each other almost every day on my way to dinner. She was seventeen, and with her firmly supple body, thin face, and fresh skin, she radiated the same quietly soulful beauty with which all her ancestors were endowed and which her mother possesses to this day. This ancient and blessed family for generations produced a line of women who were quiet and distinguished, with blooming health and flawless beauty. There exists a sixteenth-century portrait by an unknown master of a daughter of the Fugger family, one of the most delicious paintings I know: the Girtanner women all bore some resemblance to her, including Rösi.

Of course, I was unaware of this likeness at that time. I simply watched her as she walked by in her gay dignity, and I sensed the nobility and simplicity of her character. I would sit pensively in the dusk until I succeeded in conjuring up a clear image of her. Then an uncannily sweet shudder would shake my boyish soul.

Before long these moments of joy became overcast and cost me bitter pain. I suddenly realized that she was a stranger: she neither knew me nor asked about me. My beautiful vision was in fact a theft; I stole a part of her blessed being. When I felt this with most acute agony, I beheld her presence so distinctly and breathtakingly alive that a warm wave of darkness flooded my heart, making every nerve ache.

In the daytime this wave would suddenly overwhelm me in the middle of class, or even in the middle of a fight. I would close my eyes, lower my arms, and feel myself slipping into a warm abyss, until the teacher's voice or a classmate's fist woke me out of my reverie. I became withdrawn. I would run out into the open and gaze with astonished dreaminess at the world. Now I discovered how beautiful and varicolored everything was, how all things were suffused with light and breath, how clear and green the river was, how red the roofs were, and how blue the mountains. This beauty did not divert my attention; I only savored it quietly and sadly. The more beautiful everything was, the more alien it seemed, as I had no part in it and stood at its edge. In this benumbed state, my thoughts would gradually find their way back to Rösi: if I were to die at this very moment, she would not know, would not ask, or be distressed.

Yet I felt no wish to be noticed by her. I would gladly have done something unheard of, performed some feat in her behalf, or presented her with a gift without her ever knowing who had given it. In fact, I did do great things in her behalf. During a short vacation I went home and performed any number of feats of prowess every day, all of them, I felt, in Rösi's honor and glory: I climbed a difficult peak from its steepest side; I took extended trips with the skiff, covering great distances in a short time. Returning burnt out and famished from one of these excursions, it occurred to me to go without food and drink until evening, all for the sake of Rösi Girtanner. I carried her name and praise to out-of-the-way summits and ravines where no human had ever set foot.

I was also making up for the time my youthful body

had spent squatting in stuffy schoolrooms. My shoulders broadened, my face and neck became tanned, and my muscles swelled and became taut.

On the next to last day of vacation, I went to extreme pains to gather my love a floral sacrifice. I knew of several dangerous slopes covered with edelweiss, but this odorless, colorless, sickly silver flower had always seemed to me lacking in soul and beauty. Instead, I decided on some bushes of rhododendron, the "Alpine rose," which had been blown by the wind into a secluded cleft on a steep precipice. They had blossomed late and could not be more difficult to reach. But I had to find a way and, since nothing is unattainable to youth and love, I finally did reach my goal—with sore hands and feet. Shouting for joy was out of the question in the position I was in, but my heart yodeled and leaped deliriously as I snipped the tough stems and held the booty in my hand. The descent had to be accomplished by climbing backwards, the flowers between my teeth, and heaven only knows how I reached the foot of the precipice in one piece. Since all other rhododendron on the mountain had withered long before, I held the season's last in my hand, just budding and breaking into delicate bloom.

Next day I did not put down the flowers even for a moment throughout the entire five-hour trip. As I approached my sweetheart's city, my heart at first beat with excitement. Yet the farther the Alps receded, the more my inborn love drew me back to them. The Sennalpstock had long faded from view when the jagged foothills disappeared, sinking away one after another, each one detaching itself with a delicate woe from my heart. Now all the hills of my homeland had vanished and a broad, undulating, light-green lowland-scape thrust itself into view. This sight had not affected me on my first trip away from home. Today uneasiness, fear, and sadness overcame me—as though I were destined to travel into flatter and flatter lands, to lose the mountains and citizenship of my native land forever. Simultaneously I beheld the beautiful face of my Rösi, so delicate, alien, cool, and unconcerned that the bitterness and anguish of it took my breath away. The glad, spotless villages with slender spires and white gables slipped past the window; people mounted and dismounted, jabbered, laughed, smoked, made jokes—all of them cheerful lowlanders, clever, open-minded, smart people—and I, a stolid mountain youth, sat morose and silent among them. I felt not at home here, I felt permanently kidnapped from my mountain region and certain that I would never be as cheerful, smooth, and self-assured as anyone from the lowland. They would always be able to make fun of me; one of them would marry the Girtanner girl, and one of them would always stand in my way, be a step ahead of me.

Such were the thoughts that were with me on my way into town. There, after a brief look around, I climbed to my room in the attic, opened my foot locker, and took out a large sheet of wrapping paper. When I had wrapped my flowers in it and tied the package together with a string I had brought with me for that purpose, the parcel did not look at all like a gift of love. I solemnly carried it to the street where lawyer Girtanner lived and at the first opportune moment I stepped through the open door, glanced briefly into the dimly lit hallway, and deposited the ill-shaped bundle on the wide staircase.

No one saw me and I never found out if Rösi received my greeting. But I had the satisfaction of having climbed a steep precipice, of having risked my life to place a spray of rhododendron on a staircase. This knowledge contained something sweet, melancholy, and poetic, which made me feel very good; I can feel it even today. Only in times of complete despair does it occur to me that this "adventure with the Alpine roses" might have been as quixotic as all my other love affairs.

This, my first love, never came to any conclusion— its echo receded gradually and enigmatically. Unrelieved throughout my adolescence, it always accompanied me whenever I fell in love later on, like a quiet elder sister. Nor have I ever been able to imagine anything purer, lovelier, or more beautiful than that well-born, calm-eyed patrician's daughter. Many years later, when I happened to see the anonymous, enigmatic portrait of the Fugger daughter at an exhibition in Munich, it seemed to me that my whole enthusiastic, melancholy youth stood before me, gazing forlornly from the depths of its unfathomable eyes.

Meanwhile I slowly and cautiously sloughed off the skin of childhood and gradually turned into a youth. The photograph taken of me at that time shows a bony, overgrown farm boy in shabby clothes, somewhat dull-eyed, with ill-proportioned, loutish limbs. Only the head reveals a certain precocity and firmness. With a kind of astonishment, I watched myself discard my boyhood ways. I looked forward to the university with somber anticipation.

I was to study in Zurich and, in the event of my doing particularly well, my patrons held out the possibility of an extended educational tour through Europe. All this appeared to me as a beautiful classical picture: I visualized myself sitting in a friendly grove solemnly appointed with the busts of Plato and Homer, bent over learned tomes, and on all sides an unhampered view over the town, the lake and mountains, enchanting vistas. I had become a little less confused, yet livelier too, and looked forward to the good fortune awaiting me with the firm conviction that I would prove worthy of it.

During my last year at school I took up the study of Italian and made my first acquaintance with the old novelists of Italy. I promised myself a more thorough acquaintance with them as a bonus for my first year at the university. Then the day came when I said goodbye to my teachers and my housemaster, packed and secured my little foot locker, and, with pleasurably melancholy feelings, spent some time lounging about in the vicinity of Rösi's house.

The vacation that now followed gave me a bitter foretaste of life and made a mockery of my high-flown dreams. The first shock was finding my mother ill. She was bedridden, hardly spoke at all, and even my arrival did not bestir her. I did not exactly feel sorry for myself, but it hurt to find that my happiness and young pride elicited no response. Thereupon my father informed me that although he had no objections to my studying, he was in no position to help financially. If my small scholarship did not suffice, I would have to try to earn the rest myself. By the time he was my age he had eaten bread earned with his own two hands, and so forth . . .

Neither did I have much chance to go hiking, boating, or mountain-climbing, for I had to help out in the house and in the fields. During my half-days off, I did not feel like doing anything at all, not even reading. It enraged and exhausted me to observe how the common daily life callously demanded its due and devoured the abundance of optimism I had brought with me. My father, once he had settled the question of money, was as curt and harsh as ever, but not actually unfriendly. Yet this did not make me any happier. The silent, half-contemptuous respect my education and bookishness elicited from him irked me, and I felt sorry that it did. Moreover, I often thought of Rösi and was again overcome by the evil, indignant realization of my peasant inability to turn myself into a self-assured man of the world. For days I would ponder whether it might not be better to stay home and forget about Latin, burying all my hopes in the depressing regimentation of my miserable life at home. I went about tormented and wretched; I found no solace at the bedside of my sick mother. The picture of that imaginary grove with the busts of Plato and Homer rose up to mock me, and I destroyed it, heaping upon it all the scorn and venom of my tortured being. The weeks became unbearably drawn out, as though I were destined to lose my entire youth to this period of anger and frustration.

If the rashness and thoroughness with which life destroyed my blissful dreams stunned and outraged me, I was now amazed how suddenly even such agonies as these could be overcome. Life had shown me its gray work-a-day side; it now suddenly opened its infinite depths to my riveted eye and laid the burden of experience with sobering effect upon my young heart.

While still in bed, early one hot summer morning, I

felt thirsty. As I passed through my parents' bedroom
on my way to the kitchen, I heard my mother groaning.
I went up to her bed. She neither noticed nor answered
me and continued to make the same dry, frightening
moans. Her eyelids quivered and her face had a bluish
pallor. Though anxious, I was not frightened until I
noticed her hands lying on the sheet as motionless as
sleeping twins. These hands told me that my mother
was dying: they seemed so sapped of all life, so deathly
weary as no living persons. I forgot my thirst and,
kneeling down beside her, placed one hand on her
forehead and tried to catch her eyes. When our gaze
met, hers was steadfast and untroubled but nearly
extinct. It did not occur to me to wake my father, who
lay nearby, breathing heavily. I knelt there for nearly
two hours and watched my mother die. Her death took
place with calm gravity and with courage, as befitted
her kind. She set me a noble example.

The little room was quiet. Gradually it filled with the
light of the new day; house and village lay asleep, and I
had ample time to let my thoughts accompany my
dying mother's soul over house and village and lake and
snow-capped peaks into the cool freedom of a pure,
early-morning sky. I felt little grief, for I was overcome
with amazement and awe at being allowed to watch the
great riddle solve itself and the circle of life close with a
gentle tremor. The uncomplaining courage of the de-

parting spirit was so exalted that some of its simple
glory fell upon my soul as well, like a cool clear ray. My
father asleep beside her, the absence of a priest, the
homing soul not consecrated by either prayer or sacra-
ment—none of this bothered me. I felt only an ominous
breath of eternity suffuse the dawn-lit room and mingle
with my being.

At the very last moment—there was no light left in
her eyes—I kissed my mother's wilted cool lips, for the
first time in my life. The strange chill of this contact
filled me with sudden dread. I sat on the edge of the bed
and felt tear after tear glide slowly, hesitantly down my
cheeks, chin, and hands.

Then my father awoke, saw me sitting there and,
still half asleep, asked me what was wrong. I wanted to
reply but was unable to utter a word. I left him and
reached my room in a daze. I dressed slowly and me-
chanically. Soon my father appeared.

"She is dead," he said. "Did you know?"

I nodded.

"Then why did you let me go on sleeping? And no
priest attended her. May you be . . ." He uttered a
grievous curse.

At that point I felt an indefinable jab of pain in my
head, as though a vein had burst. I stepped up to him,
firmly grasped both his hands—his strength was a
boy's compared to mine—and stared him in the face. I

could not say anything, but he became still and timid. When we both went to attend to my mother, the presence of death took hold of him too and made his face strange and solemn. Then he bent down over the corpse and began lamenting softly, childlike, in high, feeble tones, almost like a bird.

I left him and went to tell the neighbors. They listened to me, asked no questions, shook my hand, and offered their help to our orphaned household. One of them went off to the monastery to fetch a priest. When I returned, I found a woman in our stable milking the cow.

The reverend father appeared, as did almost all the women of the village, and everything went off punctually and correctly as if of its own accord. Even the coffin materialized without our having to lift a hand, and I could see clearly for the first time in my life how good it is, during difficult times, to be among one's own people and to be one of a small, self-sufficient community. Perhaps I ought to have thought about this more deeply. For the next day, once the coffin had been blessed and lowered and the odd assemblage of woefully old-fashioned, bristly top hats—including my father's—had disappeared each into its own box and cupboard, my father was seized with a fit of weakness. All at once he began feeling sorry for himself, bemoaning his misery in strange, largely Biblical, phrases, complaining to me that now that his wife was buried he would also lose his son. There was no stopping it. Startled, I listened and was on the point of promising him I would stay when—my lips were already parted—something very odd happened.

Everything I had thought and desired and longed for since childhood appeared for a brief second before my mind's eye. I saw great, beautiful tasks awaiting me, books I would read and books I would write. I heard the Föhn sweep by, and saw distant blissful lakes and shores bathed in southern lights and colors. I saw people with intelligent, cultured faces walking past; I saw elegantly beautiful women; I saw streets, mountain passes leading over the Alps, and trains hurrying from one country to the next—all this I beheld simultaneously, yet each part separately and distinctly. Behind all of it was the boundless spread of a clear horizon dotted with clouds. Learning, creating, seeing, voyaging—the abundance of life flared up in a fleeting silver gleam before my eyes. And once again, as in my boyhood, something trembled within me, a mighty, unconscious force straining toward the great distances of the world.

I said nothing and let my father talk on, shaking my head every so often, waiting for his impetuousness to subside. This happened toward evening. Then I explained to him my irrevocable decision to study and to seek my future home in the realm of intellect—without, however, asking any support from him. He stopped cajoling at this point and looked at me pitifully, shaking his head. For he realized that I would go my own way from now on, and would soon be completely estranged from his way of life. As I write this, I can see my father exactly as he sat that evening in the chair by the window: his chiseled, shrewd peasant head motionless on the lean neck, his short hair beginning to turn gray, his severe and simple features betraying the struggle his tough masculinity was waging against grief and the onset of old age.

Of these days a small but significant event remains to be told. One evening, about a week before my departure, my father put on his cap.

"Where are you off to?" I asked.

"Is that any of your business?"

"Well, you could tell me, if it's not illegal."

Whereupon he laughed and called out: "No reason why you shouldn't come along. You're no child any more." So we both went off to the tavern. A few farmers were sitting in front of a jug of Hallauer, two wagoners whom I did not know were drinking absinthe, and a tableful of young fellows were conducting a noisy session of a card game called jass.

I was used to drinking an occasional glass of wine, but this was the first time I had entered a tavern without actually being thirsty. I knew from hearsay that my father was an accomplished drinker. He drank heavily, and only the best, and consequently his household, though he could not be said seriously to neglect it otherwise, had floundered in a perpetual state of misery. I was impressed by how respectfully the innkeeper and the other guests treated him. He ordered a liter of Vaud, bade me pour it, and demonstrated the correct manner of doing so. You have to begin pouring at a low angle, gradually lengthening the jet, and bringing the bottle down as low as possible at the end. Then he began telling me about the different wines he knew, wines he enjoyed on the rare occasions when he ventured to town or over the border to the Italian side. He spoke with deep respect of the dark-red Veltliner and then proceeded to discourse in low, urgent tones about certain bottled Vaud wines; finally, almost in a whisper and with the expression of someone recounting a fairy tale, he spoke to me of the Neuchâtels. The foam of certain vintages assumed the shape of a star on being poured, and he drew a star on the table with a wet finger. Then he entered into profound speculation as to the nature and flavor of champagne, which he had never tasted, and one bottle of which he believed could make two men stark raving drunk.

Falling silent and pensive, he lit his pipe. Noticing that I had nothing to smoke, he gave me ten centimes for cigars. Then we sat opposite each other, blowing smoke into each other's faces and slowly gulping down the first liter of wine. The golden, piquant Vaud was excellent. Gradually the farmers at the next table ventured to join in our conversation and eventually came over to join us—one by one, carefully and with much self-conscious throat-clearing. It was not long before I was the center of attention, and it became evident that I had a fantastic reputation as a mountain climber. All manner of foolhardy ascents and spectacular falls, enshrouded in myth, were recounted, disputed, and defended. Meanwhile, we had almost drained our second measure of wine. The blood was now rushing to my head and uncharacteristically I began to boast, telling of the hazardous climb along the upper wall of the Sennalpstock where I had fetched Rösi Girtanner's roses. They refused to believe me, I protested, they laughed, and I became furious. I challenged anyone who disbelieved me to a wrestling match and informed them that I could take care of the whole lot of them. Thereupon a bandy-legged old farmer walked over to one of the shelves and brought back a huge earthenware jug, placing it on its side on the table.

"I'll tell you something," he said. "If you're all that strong, why don't you smash that jug with your fist? Then we'll pay for as much wine as it holds. And if you can't do it, you'll pay for the wine."

My father agreed to it at once. I stood up, wrapped my handkerchief around my hand, and struck. The first two blows had no effect. With the third, the jug shattered. "Pay up," crowed my father, beaming with delight, and the old farmer seemed to have no objections. "Fine," he said. "I'll pay for as much wine as the jug takes. But that won't be much any more." Naturally the shards would not hold even a measure, and so I had to accept their kidding as the only return for the pain in my arm. Even my father was laughing at me now.

"Well then, you've won," I shouted and, filling the biggest of the shards with wine from our bottle, poured it over the old man's bald pate. Now *we* had won and the guests applauded.

Further horseplay of this sort followed. Then my father lugged me home and we stumbled excitedly and roughly through the room in which my mother's coffin had rested less than three weeks before. I slept as if dead and felt like a complete wreck the next morning. My father taunted me and carried on his activities, pleased by his obvious superiority as a drinker. I silently made a vow never to go drinking again and longed for the day of my departure.

Finally it came and I left, but I did not keep my vow. The golden Vaud, the dark-red Veltliner, the Neuchâtel, and many other wines and I began a long acquaintance and have become the best of friends since.

Chapter Three

DRESSED IN A NEW BUCKSKIN SUIT and carrying a small chest filled with books and other possessions, I arrived in Zurich, ready to conquer a piece of the world and to prove as quickly as possible to the roughnecks back home that I was made of different stuff from the other Camenzinds. For three wonderful years I lived in the same drafty attic with its commanding view, studied, wrote poems, longed for and sensed myself imbued with everything that is beautiful on earth. Although I did not have a hot meal every day of the week, every day and every night my heart sang and laughed and wept with joy and cleaved fervently, longingly to life.

This was my first real city. Greenhorn that I was, I walked about wide-eyed and bewildered for several weeks. It never occurred to me to admire genuinely or be envious of city life—I was too much of a farm boy for that—but the multitude of streets, houses, and people delighted me. I observed how alive with carriages the streets were; I inspected the moorings on the lake, the plazas, the gardens, the ostentatious civic buildings and churches; I saw crowds hurry off to work, students dawdling, the well-to-do on outings, dandies preening themselves, foreigners ambling aimlessly about. The fashionably elegant and haughty wives of the rich seemed to me like peacocks in a chicken yard, pretty, proud, and a little foolish. No, I was not really shy—only awkward and stubborn—and I had no doubts that I was man enough to become thoroughly acquainted with this lively city and to make my way in it.

Making the acquaintance of a handsome young fellow who lived in two rooms on the second floor of my house, and who was also a student in Zurich, was the first move I made in this direction. Actually I did not take this step myself, for he came up to me. I heard him practicing the piano every day, and listening to him, I felt for the first time something of the magic of music, the most feminine, the sweetest of the arts. I would watch him leave the house, with a book or a score in his left hand, in his right a cigarette whose smoke trailed behind him as he walked off with easy and graceful steps. I was fascinated but I kept my distance. I was afraid of making the acquaintance of someone so easygoing, free, and well-to-do, fearing it would only humiliate me and underscore my poverty and rough manners. Then he came up to see me: one evening there was a knock on my door. I was startled, for no one had called on me before. He entered, shook my hand, introduced himself, and his behavior was as easy and natural as though we had known each other for years.

"I wanted to ask whether you would like to play some music with me," he said. I had never touched an instrument, much less played one. I told him this, adding that except for yodeling I was without art but that his piano playing had often drifted pleasurably and temptingly up to my room.

"How wrong can you be!" he exclaimed. "Judging from your looks, I could have sworn that you were a musician. Very strange. But you can yodel. Then you must yodel for me. Please, just once. I love the sound of it."

I was dismayed at the thought and explained that it was impossible for me to yodel to order. It was only possible on a mountain top, at least out in the open air, and it would have to come spontaneously.

"Well then, yodel on a mountain. Is tomorrow all right with you? We could go for a walk somewhere, toward evening. Just walk about, talk a little, climb some mountain, and then you can yodel to your heart's delight. Afterwards we can go eat at some village inn. You have the time, don't you?"

Oh, yes, I had all the time in the world and I quickly consented. Then I asked him to play something for me and we went downstairs into his large, well-furnished·

apartment. A few paintings in modern frames, a piano, a certain decorative disorder, and the smell of expensive cigarettes produced an atmosphere of comfortable and relaxing elegance that was quite new to me. Richard sat down at the piano and played a few bars.

"You know what that is, don't you?" he said, nodding in my direction. He looked quite extraordinary, turning his head away from the keyboard, his eyes glowing.

"No," I said, "I don't know anything about music."

"It's Wagner," he called back. "It's from *Die Meistersinger*." And he continued playing. The music sounded light and vigorous, longing and exuberant, and I felt as though immersed in a warm, effervescent bath. Looking with secret joy at his neck, at the backs of his pale musician's hands, I was overcome by the same feeling of tenderness and respect with which I had once looked at the dark-haired student from my schooldays, as well as by the shy premonition that this handsome, distinguished person might really become my friend and make my old but unforgotten wish for such a friendship come true.

Next day I went to get him. Slowly, and talking all the way, we climbed to the top of a medium-sized hill and gained a view of the city, the lake, and the gardens and savored the rich beauty of early evening.

"And now you can yodel," said Richard. "If you're still embarrassed, turn your back to me. But loud, if you please."

He should have been well satisfied. I yodeled madly, exultantly, with every possible break and variation, into the shimmering evening. When I stopped, he started to say something, then just cocked his ear in the direction of the mountains. From a distant peak there came a reply, soft and long-drawn-out and swelling gradually, a herdsman's or a hiker's answer, and we listened quietly and happily to it. As we stood there listening, I became aware for the first time in my life of the delight of standing alongside a friend, gazing together into the remote and hazy vistas of life. In the evening light, the lake came alive with a soft play of colors. Shortly before sunset I noticed a few stubborn, impudently jagged peaks jutting through the dissolving mist.

"That's where my home is," I said. "The peak in the middle is the Rote Fluh; on its right is the Geisshorn; and farther off to the left is the Sennalpstock, which is rounded on top. I was ten years and three weeks old the first time I stood on its top."

I strained my eyes to make out one of the peaks farther south. After a while Richard said something that I did not hear clearly.

"What did you say?" I asked.

"I said I now know your gift."

"What's that?"

"You're a poet."

At this point I blushed and became angry. I was amazed that he had guessed.

"No," I exclaimed. "I'm not a poet. I did in fact write a few verses when I was in school, but I haven't written anything for a long time."

"Would you show them to me?"

"I've burned them. But even if I hadn't, I wouldn't show them to you."

"They must have been very modern, with a lot of Nietzsche in them, I imagine."

"Who's he?"

"Nietzsche? My God, here's a fellow who doesn't know Nietzsche!"

"No. How could I?"

He was delighted that I did not know Nietzsche, and I became furious and asked him how many glaciers he had scaled. When he said he hadn't scaled any, I teased him as much as he had teased me. Then he put his hand on my shoulder and said in a very serious tone of voice: "You are touchy. But you've no idea how enviably unspoiled you are, and how few people like you there are on this earth. Look, in a year or so you'll know all about Nietzsche and more and you'll know it much better than I ever will, because you're more thorough and brighter than I. But I like you the way you are now. You don't know Nietzsche and Wagner but you've climbed mountains and you have such a sturdy mountain face. And there's absolutely no doubt that you're a poet. I can see it from your glance and your forehead."

I was amazed that he should look at me so directly

and express his views with such frankness and lack of embarrassment. It struck me as most unusual. I was even more astonished and delighted when a week later, in a very crowded beer-garden, he swore eternal friendship, jumped up and embraced me and kissed me in front of all the customers, and then danced me around the table as though he were mad.

"What will people think?" I tried to admonish him.

"They'll think: those two are extraordinarily happy or more than extraordinarily drunk. But most of them won't give it any thought at all."

Though he was older, cleverer, better brought up, and better versed in everything than I, he seemed often a mere child in comparison. On the street, for instance, he would suddenly flirt half-mockingly with teenage girls or he would interrupt the most serious piece of music with a childish joke. On one occasion when we had gone to church he suddenly whispered to me in the middle of the sermon: "Don't you find that the priest looks like a wizened rabbit?" The comparison was perfect but I felt he could just as well have pointed it out after church and I later told him so.

"But it was true, wasn't it?" he grumbled. "I probably would not have remembered it afterward."

It did not bother me or others when his jokes fell flat or were little more than quotes from a book. What we liked about him was not his wit and intelligence, but his free and lighthearted air and the irrepressible gaiety of his transparently childish nature, which could break forth at any moment.

Richard often took me along when he went to meet other people our age—students, musicians, painters, writers, and foreigners of all sorts. All the interesting, art-loving, unusual persons in town eventually made his acquaintance. Among them there were very serious, deeply committed people—philosophers, aestheticians, socialists—and I was able to learn something from all of them. Bits of knowledge from a wide variety of fields came my way and I tried to supplement them by much reading on the side. I gradually gained a fairly clear notion of what fascinated and tormented the liveliest spirits of the day and, moreover, gained stimulating insights into the wishes, premonitions, achievements, and ideals of the intellectuals. These attracted me and I understood them, but I myself lacked any strong urge to take sides on any of the issues, either pro or con. I discovered that in most cases the intellectual fervor was directed at analyzing the conditions and the structure of society and the state, at the sciences, the arts, and at teaching methods. Yet only a small minority seemed aware of the need to develop their own selves and to clarify their personal relationship to time and eternity. And in my case, the awareness of this need was not very great at that time.

I made no further friends because of my exclusive

and jealous affection for Richard. This was so exclusive that I even tried to draw him away from the many women he knew. When we arranged to meet, I was always scrupulously punctual, however unimportant the event, and I was very touchy if he kept me waiting. Once he asked me to call for him at a certain hour to go rowing. I did not find him home and waited three hours. The next day I reproached him bitterly.

"Why didn't you go rowing by yourself?" he laughed. 'I'd completely forgotten about it. That isn't a catastrophe, is it?"

"I'm accustomed to keeping promises to the letter," I replied heatedly and pompously. "But of course by now I'm used to its not mattering to you at all that you keep me waiting—not if one has as many friends as you . . ."

He looked at me with immense astonishment. "Do you take trifles like that seriously?"

"My friendship is more than a trifle to me."

> *"This saying made such deep impress*
> *That he swiftly swore redress . . ."*

Richard quoted solemnly. He seized my hand and rubbed his nose affectionately against mine in Eskimo fashion, until I freed myself from him with an angry laugh. But the friendship had been repaired.

Modern philosophers, poets, critics—in borrowed, often expensive editions—literary reviews from Germany and France, new plays, Parisian *feuilletons*, and the works of the fashionable Viennese aestheticians were all piled up in my attic. I read them quickly but reserved most of my attention for my old Italian novelists and my historical studies. I wanted to have done with philology as soon as possible and devote myself exclusively to history. Besides works on general history and historical methodology, I read sources and monographs about the late Middle Ages in Italy and France, and in this reading I made my first acquaintance with my favorite among men, the most godly and most blessed of saints, Francis of Assisi.

That dream of mine which had shown me the splendor of life and intellect came true each day and warmed my heart with ambition, joy, and youthful vanity. In the lecture halls I had to pay attention to serious, rather dry, and occasionally somewhat tedious scholarship. At home I returned to the intimate and devout or gruesome tales of the Middle Ages, or to the more leisurely old storytellers whose beautiful and well-appointed world harbored me as if I were in a shadowy enchanted corner. Or I felt the wild wave of modern ideals and passions sweep over me. In between I would listen to music, laugh with Richard, be with him and his friends, meet Frenchmen, Germans, and Russians, listen to strange modern books being read aloud, visit painters' studios or attend soirees at which crowds of excited and muddled intellectuals surrounded me as if at some fantastic carnival.

One Sunday when Richard and I were visiting a small exhibition of new paintings, my friend stopped short before a picture of a mountain with a few goats on its slope. It was carefully and nicely executed, but it was a little old-fashioned and lacked artistry. You can find pretty, relatively trivial paintings like this in every salon, but still this painting pleased me because it was a fairly accurate rendering of the meadows where I grew up. I asked Richard what had attracted him to the picture.

"This," he said, pointing to the signature in the corner. I could not decipher the reddish-brown letters. "The painting," Richard continued, "is no great achievement—any number like it are more beautiful—but there is no painter more beautiful than the woman who painted it. Her name is Erminia Aglietti, and if you like we can call on her tomorrow and tell her she's a great painter."

"Then you know her?"

"Yes. If her paintings were as beautiful as she is, she would be wealthy and would not be painting any more. For she does not enjoy it and paints only because she happens not to have learned any other way to make a living."

Richard forgot all about it and did not mention her

again until a few weeks later. "I ran into the Aglietti girl yesterday. We were going to visit her a couple of weeks back, you remember. Come on. Your collar is clean, isn't it? She's a bit finicky about that."

My shirt was clean and we went off to see the Aglietti girl, I not without misgivings, for the rather rough and ready relationship of Richard and his friends with women painters and students had never appealed to me. The men were quite ruthless—sometimes coarse, sometimes sarcastic; the girls, on the other hand, were practical, clever, and shrewd—and devoid of the ethereal haze in which I preferred to see and venerate women.

I entered the studio feeling somewhat apprehensive. I was used to the atmosphere of painters' workshops, but this was my first time in a woman's studio. It made a simple, well-ordered impression. Three or four finished paintings hung in their frames; another, on which she had just begun, stood on the easel. The other walls were covered with neat, attractive pencil sketches. There was also a half-filled bookcase. The painter coolly accepted our greeting. She laid down her brush and leaned against the bookcase in her smock, looking as though she did not want to waste much time on us.

Richard showered her with extravagant praise of the picture we had seen at the exhibition. She laughed and cut him short.

"But I might want to buy the painting. Besides, the cows in it are so true to life . . ."

"But they're goats," she said quietly.

"Goats? Of course, goats. Observed with an accuracy that is absolutely breathtaking. They are about to leap off the canvas, completely goatlike. Just ask my friend Camenzind, a son of the mountains himself. He'll back me up."

I felt the painter's eye sweep over me critically, while I listened with a mixture of embarrassment and amusement to the banter. She looked at me for some time, quite uninhibitedly.

"You are from the mountains?"

"Yes."

"It's obvious. Well, how do you feel about my goats?"

"Oh, they're excellent. I certainly never thought they were cows as Richard did."

"Very nice of you to say so. Are you a musician?"

"No, a student."

She said nothing further to me and now I had a chance to observe her. Her long painter's smock hid and distorted her figure, and her face did not strike me as beautiful. The features were sharp and sparse; the eyes a little hard; the hair full, black, and soft. What bothered me—almost repelled me—was her complexion: it made me think at once of Gorgonzola; I would not have been surprised to find greenish veins in it. I had not seen this Italian paleness before, and now, in the unfavorable morning light of the studio, her skin looked startlingly like stone—not marble, but like some weathered, highly bleached stone. And I was not in the habit of testing a woman's face by its shape but was accustomed—still in my somewhat boyish fashion—to look for softness, hue, and loveliness of complexion.

The visit had put Richard in a bad mood too, so I was astonished, actually frightened, when he said sometime afterwards that the Aglietti girl would like to do a drawing of me. It would only be a sketch; she was not interested in my face but in my "typical" broad massive figure.

Before we had a chance to discuss this at greater length, something occurred which transformed my life and set my future course for many years. Suddenly, when I awoke one morning, I was a writer.

At Richard's urging I had occasionally written brief sketches and portraits of types in our circle and also a few essays on literary and historical subjects—all of them as accurate as possible, but purely stylistic exercises.

One morning, when I was still in bed, Richard came in and placed thirty-five francs on my blanket. "They are yours," he said in a businesslike voice. Finally, after I had exhausted all possible explanations, he drew a page of a newspaper out of his pocket and showed me one of my essays printed there. He had copied a number of my manuscripts and taken them to an editor friend and sold them quietly behind my back. I now held the first piece the editor had bought, as well as the fee.

I had never felt as strange as I did then. Although I was furious that Richard should have assumed such a providential role, the first sweet pride in being a writer and having earned the money, and the thought of a certain, though small, literary fame, overcame my irritation.

Richard had me meet the editor in a café. The editor asked if he might keep the other pieces Richard had shown him and asked me to send more. He said my pieces had a distinctive tone, particularly those on historical subjects, and he would be glad to have more in the same vein and would pay a good fee. Only then did I fully grasp what had happened. Not only would I be able to eat regularly and settle my small debts, but I could abandon the course of studies I'd been compelled to follow and might even be able to afford working solely in my chosen field.

Meanwhile, the editor had a batch of new books sent to my place for review. I worked my way through these and was kept busy for several weeks. Since payments were due at the end of the quarter and I had exceeded my usual standard of living in anticipation of this income, one day I found myself without a centime to my name and was forced to go hungry again. For a few days I held out in my attic on a diet of bread and coffee, then hunger pangs drove me out to a restaurant. I took three books along to leave as security in lieu of payment, having already made a vain attempt to sell them at a secondhand bookshop. The meal was first-rate. Only after I drank my cup of black coffee did I begin to feel uneasy.

With some trepidation, I confessed to the waitress that I was broke. Couldn't I leave the books instead? She picked one of them up from the table—a volume of poetry—leafed through it with evident curiosity, and asked whether she could read it. She liked reading, she said, but somehow never had the chance to get hold of good books. Then I knew I was saved. I suggested that she take all three books as payment for my meal. She accepted and over a period of time took seventeen francs' worth of books off my hands. For a slim volume of poetry, I demanded a cheese sandwich; for a novel, the same plus a glass of wine; a single novella was worth a cup of coffee and a serving of bread.

As I remember, these were all quite insignificant books written in a painfully cramped, fashionable style, so the goodhearted girl probably received a strange impression of modern German literature. With real delight I can recollect mornings on which I would race through a book, scribble a few lines of comment so

I would be done with it by noon, and take it to trade in for lunch. But I took pains to hide my financial difficulties from Richard, for I felt unnecessarily ashamed and disliked accepting his help except in the most dire circumstances.

I did not think of myself as a poet. What I wrote on occasion was *feuilleton* stuff, not poetry. Yet I cherished the hope that one day I would succeed in creating a work of literature, a great, proud song of longing and of life.

The clear, lighthearted mirror of my soul was overcast at times by a kind of melancholy. Yet it was not seriously ruffled at first. These shadows appeared for a day or a night in the form of dreamy, forlorn sadness, then disappeared again without a trace, only to return suddenly after weeks or months. I got used to this sadness as to a mistress. I did not feel tortured but experienced an uneasy weariness that had a certain sweetness all its own. If this melancholy enveloped me at night, I would lie for hours by the window gazing down upon the black lake and up at the mountains silhouetted against the wan sky, with stars suspended above. Then a fearfully sweet, overpowering emotion would take hold of me—as though all the nighttime beauty looked at me accusingly, stars and mountain and lake longing for someone who understood the beauty and agony of their mute existence, who could express it for them, as though I were the one meant to do this and as though my true calling were to give expression to inarticulate nature in poems.

I never gave any thought to how I would go about doing this; I only sensed the beautiful grave night mutely longing for me. And I never wrote a poem when I was in such a mood, though I felt responsible for these dark voices and usually would set out on an extended solitary walk after one of these nights. I felt that in this fashion I requited a little the earth's love which offered itself up to me in silent supplication, an idea I could only laugh at afterward. These walks, however, became one of the bases of my later life, large parts of which I have spent as a wanderer, hiking for weeks and months from country to country. I grew used to tramping on, with only a little money and a crust of bread in my pockets, to being by myself for days on end and spending nights out in the open.

I had forgotten the Aglietti girl now that I was becoming a writer. Then she sent a note: "I'm giving a tea on Thursday at my place. Why don't you come and bring your friend?"

Richard and I went and found there a small coterie of artists. For the most part they were unrecognized, forgotten, or unsuccessful, which I found touching, although all of them seemed quite contented and merry. We were given tea, sandwiches, ham, and a salad. Because I didn't know any of the people and was not gregarious anyway, I gave in to my hunger pangs and for an hour did little but eat, quietly and persistently, while the others sipped their tea and chattered. By the time they were ready for food, I'd consumed almost half the ham. I'd assured myself that there would be at least another platter in reserve. They all chuckled softly and I reaped a few glances so ironical that I became furious and damned the Italian girl as well as her ham, rose to my feet, and excused myself, explaining curtly that I would bring my own dinner along the next time. Then I reached for my hat.

The Aglietti girl took back my hat, looked astonished at me, and begged me to stay. The soft lamplight fell on her face and I was struck by the wonderfully mature beauty of this woman. I suddenly felt very stupid and naughty, like a school boy who has been reprimanded, and I sat down again in a far corner of the room. There I stayed, leafing through a picture album of Lake Como. The others went on sipping their tea, paced back and forth, laughed, and talked. Nearby a cello and violins were tuning up. A curtain was drawn aside and I could see four musicians at improvised stands ready to perform a string quartet. Erminia came toward me, placed her cup on a side table, nodded kindly, and sat down beside me. The quartet played for some time, but I did not listen closely. I gazed with growing amazement at

the slender, elegant woman whose beauty I had
doubted and whose refreshments I had gobbled up.
With mixed feelings of joy and apprehension, I now
remembered that she had wanted to draw me. Then my
thoughts returned to Rösi Girtanner, for whom I had
climbed after rhododendron, and to the fable of the
Snow Princess, all of which now seemed to me to have
been preparation for the present moment.

When the music ended, Erminia did not leave me as
I had feared she would, but sat quietly beside me and
then began to talk. She congratulated me on one of my
pieces she had seen in the newspaper. She joked about
Richard, who was surrounded by girls and whose carefree laughter could be heard above the laughter of all
the others. When she asked again if she could paint me,
it occurred to me to continue our conversation in Italian. I was not only rewarded with a happy, surprised
glance from her vivacious Mediterranean eyes, but had
the pleasure of hearing her speak the language that
best suited her lips and eyes and figure—the euphoni-
ous, elegant, flowing lingua toscana with a charming
touch of Ticino Swiss. I myself spoke neither beautifully nor fluently, but this did not bother me at all. We
agreed I was to come and sit for her the next day.

"Arrivederla," I said as we parted, giving as deep a
bow as I could.

"Arrivederci domani," she smiled, nodding to me.

After leaving her house, I walked along the street

until it reached the ridge of a hill and I beheld the dark landscape stretched out before me in beauty's strong repose. A solitary boat with a red lantern was gliding over the lake; its blackness was broken by flickering scarlet slivers, and an occasional wave fell in a silvery silhouette. Laughter, mandolin music from a nearby beer-garden. The sky was overcast and a strong warm breeze swept across the hills.

Like the wind that caressed and shook and bent the fruit trees and the black crowns of the chestnut trees and made them moan, laugh, and quiver, so my passion played within me. On that hilltop I knelt and groveled on the ground, leaped up and groaned, stomped about, tossed away my hat, buried my face in the grass, grasped the tree trunks, cried, laughed, sobbed, raged, wept with shame, shivered with bliss, and then felt utterly crushed.

After an hour of this frenzy, all tension left me and I felt choked by a kind of sultriness. My mind went blank. I could reach no decision, I felt nothing; like a sleepwalker I descended the hill, walked aimlessly back and forth through town, found a tavern still open, entered it without any real desire, drank two full measures of wine and got home, terribly drunk, in the early morning.

Erminia was quite startled when she saw me that afternoon.

"What happened? Are you ill?"

"Nothing serious," I replied. "It seems I got very drunk last night, that's all."

She propped me on a chair and asked me not to move. Soon I dozed off and slept through the entire afternoon in her studio. Presumably it was the smell of turpentine that made me dream of our skiff back home being freshly painted. I lay on the gravel and watched my father plying the paintbrush. Mother was there too and when I asked her if she hadn't died, she replied gently: "No. For if I were not here, you'd end up like your father."

I was awakened by falling off the chair and found myself transplanted into Erminia Aglietti's studio. Though I could not see her, I gathered from the clattering of dishes and cutlery that she was preparing dinner.

"How are you?" she called to me.

"Fine. How long did I sleep?"

"Four full hours. Aren't you ashamed of yourself?"

"A little. But I had such a beautiful dream."

"Tell it to me."

"Only if you come here and forgive me."

She came but would not forgive me until I told her the dream. So I recounted it in detail and in the process plunged deeply into half-forgotten childhood memories. By the time I stopped, when it had grown dark outside, I had told her and myself the story of my childhood. She gave me her hand, smoothed my wrinkled jacket, and invited me to sit for her again the next day, so that I felt she had understood, as well as forgiven, my behavior.

Though I posed for her hour after hour during the next few days, we scarcely talked at all. I simply sat, or stood calmly, as if enchanted. I listened to the soft rasp of the charcoal and inhaled the faint smell of paint, delighting in the proximity of the woman I loved, while her eyes rested on me all the time. The white studio light bathed the walls, a few sleepy flies buzzed against the panes, and in the small room adjacent to the studio the flame hissed in the spirit lamp, for at the end of each session she served me a cup of tea.

My thoughts remained with Erminia even when I was back in my attic. It did not diminish my passion that I was unable to admire her art. She herself was so beautiful, so good and self-confident—what did her painting matter to me? On the contrary, her industry had a heroic quality: a woman battling for her livelihood, a quiet, persevering, courageous heroine.

Anyway, there's nothing more futile than ruminating about someone you love; such thoughts are like a treadmill. That is one reason why my memory of the beautiful Italian girl, though not indistinct, lacks many of the small details and features that we notice more readily in strangers than in those who are close to us. For example, I cannot remember how she wore her hair, how she dressed, and so on, or even whether she was short or tall. Whenever I think of her, I see a dark-haired, nobly shaped head, a pair of radiant eyes set in a pale, vivacious face with a beautifully shaped mouth. And when I think of her and the time I was in love with her, I always return to that night on the hill with the wind blowing over the lake and myself weeping, overjoyed, going berserk; and to one other night that I will tell of now.

It had become clear to me that I would have to make some kind of profession of love and actually woo her. If we had not seen each other almost every day, I might have been content to worship her from afar and suffer in silence. But since I saw her so frequently, talked to her, shook her hand, entered her house, my heart was in a continuous state of torment and I could not endure it for long.

Some artist friends of hers arranged a small party in a beautiful garden beside the lake on a mild mid-summer evening. We drank chilled wine, listened to music, and gazed at the red Japanese lanterns that were hung in garlands between the trees. We talked, joked, laughed, and finally burst out in song. Some fool-ish young painter was enjoying himself in the role of a romantic fop; he wore his beret at a rakish angle and lay with his back to the fence, fondling a long-necked guitar. The few artists of consequence who had been

invited had not come or else sat off to the side. Some
girls had shown up in light summer dresses; others
wore the usual unorthodox costumes. Richard flirted
with the girls, and I, despite my inner turbulence, felt
cool, drank little, and waited for Erminia, who had
promised to let me take her out in a boat. When she
arrived, she made me a present of some flowers, and
we got into a small rowboat.

The lake was as smooth as oil and as colorless as the
night. I rowed the boat swiftly out onto the calm ex-
panse, all the while gazing intently at the slender
woman leaning back comfortably and contented
against the stern. As the sky gradually darkened and
one star after another glinted through the waning blue,
the sounds of music and of people amusing themselves
on shore drifted over to us. The sluggish water accepted
the oars with gentle gurgling, and other boats drifted
about here and there almost invisible in the calm. But I
paid little heed to them. My eyes were riveted on my
companion and my thoughts were fixed on a declaration of love that clasped my anxious heart like a steel
ring. The beauty and poetry of the moment, the boat,
the stars, the tranquil lake, made me hesitant; it
seemed as though I would have to act out a sentimental
scene on a beautifully set stage. Fearful and numbed
by the profound stillness—for neither of us spoke—I
rowed as hard as I could.

"How strong you are," she said thoughtfully.

"You mean bulky, don't you?"

"No, I mean muscular," she laughed softly.

It was not a very appropriate beginning. Sadly and angrily, I continued to row. After a while I asked her to tell me something about her life.

"What would you like to hear?"

"Everything," I said. "Preferably a love story. Then I'll be able to tell you one of my own in turn. It is very brief and beautiful and it will amuse you."

"Well, let's hear it!"

"No, you first. You already know much more about me than I do about you. I would like to know if you've ever been really in love or whether—as I'm afraid—you are far too intelligent and proud for that."

Erminia pondered for a while.

"That's another of your romantic notions," she said, "to have a woman tell you stories at night in the middle of a lake. Unfortunately I can't do it. You poets are accustomed to finding words for everything beautiful and you don't even grant that people have hearts if they are less talkative about their feelings than you. Well, you couldn't be more wrong in my case, for I don't think anyone can love more passionately. I am in love with a man who is married, and he loves me just as much. Yet neither of us knows whether we will ever be able to live together. We write to each other and occasionally we meet . . ."

"Can I ask whether this love makes you happy or miserable, or both?"

"Oh, love isn't there to make us happy. I believe it exists to show us how much we can endure."

This I understood so deeply that I was unable to repress a little moan, which escaped my lips instead of a reply. She heard it.

"Ah," she said, "so you know what it's like. And you are so young still! Do you want to tell me about it now—but don't unless you really want to."

"Perhaps another time, Erminia. I don't feel up to it now and I'm sorry if I've spoiled your evening by bringing up the subject. Shall we turn back?"

"As you wish. How far from shore are we actually?"

I made no reply but dipped the oars violently into the water, swung the boat about, and pulled as though a storm were drawing near. The boat glided rapidly over the water. Amid the confusion and anguish and mortification seething within me, I felt sweat pouring down my face; I shivered at the same time. When I realized how close I had been to playing the suitor on his knees, the lover rejected with motherly and kindly understanding, a shudder ran down my spine. At least I had been spared that, and I would simply have to come to terms with my misery on my own. I rowed back like one possessed.

Erminia was somewhat taken aback when I left her as soon as we stepped on shore. The lake was as

smooth, the music as lighthearted, and the paper
moons as colorful and festive as before, yet it all seemed
stupid and ridiculous to me now. I felt like hitting the
fop in the velvet coat, who still carried his guitar osten-
tatiously on a silk band around his neck. And there
were still fireworks to come. It was all so childish.

I borrowed a few francs from Richard, pushed my
hat back, and marched off, out of town, on and on,
hour after hour until I began to feel sleepy. I lay down
in a meadow but woke again within the hour, wet with
dew, stiff, shivering with cold, and walked on to the
nearest village. It was early morning now. Reapers on
their way to mow clover were in the streets, drowsy
farmworkers stared at me wide-eyed from stable doors,
everywhere there was evidence of farmers pursuing
their summer's work. *You should have stayed a farmer,*
I told myself, and stalked shamefaced through the village and strode on until the first warmth of the sun
allowed me to rest. At the edge of a beech grove I
flopped down on the dry grass and slept in the sun until
late afternoon. When I awoke with my head full of the
aroma of the meadow and my limbs agreeably heavy,
as they can only be after lying on God's dear earth, the
fete, the trip on the lake, and the whole affair seemed
remote, sad, and half forgotten, like a novel read
months ago.

I stayed away three whole days, let the sun tan me,

and considered whether I should not head straight home—now that I was underway—and help my father bring in the second crop of hay.

Of course, my misery was not overcome as easily as all that. After I returned to the city, I fled the sight of Erminia. But it was not possible to keep this up very long. Whenever we met afterward, the misery rose up again in my throat.

Chapter Four

THE MISERY OF UNREQUITED LOVE accomplished what had been beyond my father's powers. It made me into a hardened drinker, and the effect of drink on my life has been more lasting than anything I have described so far. The strong sweet god of wine became my faithful friend, as he remains even today. Who is as mighty as he? Who as beautiful, as fantastic, lighthearted, and melancholy? He is hero and magician, tempter and brother of Eros. He can do the impossible; he imbues impoverished hearts with poetry. He transformed me, a peasant and a recluse, into a king, a poet, and a sage. He fills the emptied vessels of life with new destinies and drives the stranded back into the swift currents of action.

Such is the nature of wine. Yet, as with all delightful gifts and arts, it must be cherished, sought out, and understood at great cost and effort. Few can accomplish this feat and the god of wine vanquishes thousands upon thousands; he ages them, destroys them, or extinguishes the spirit's flame. However, he invites those who are dear to him to feast and builds them rainbow bridges to blissful isles. When they are weary, he cushions their heads; he embraces and comforts them like a mother when they become melancholy. He transforms the confusions of life into great myths and plays the hymn of creation on a mighty harp.

At other times he is childlike, with long, silky curls, narrow shoulders, and delicate limbs. He will nestle against your heart, raise his innocent face up to you, and gaze at you dreamily, astonished, out of big, fond eyes in whose depths memories of paradise and kinship with a god surge and sparkle like a forest spring. The sweet god also resembles a stream wandering with deep rushing sounds through the spring night; and resembles an ocean that cradles sun and storms in its cool waves.

When he communes with his favorites, the storm tide of secrets, memories, poetry, and premonitions floods and intoxicates them. The known world shrinks and vanishes, and the soul hurls itself with fear and joy into the uncharted distances of the unknown where everything is strange and yet familiar, and the language of music, of poets, and of dreams is spoken.

I must first recount how I discovered this secret.

Sometimes I would forget myself for hours and be perfectly happy—I would study, write, or listen to Richard play the piano. Yet not one day passed without some slight unhappiness. At times it would not overwhelm me until I had gone to bed, so that I moaned and leaped up, only to fall asleep late at night, sobbing. Or

it would stir within me after I had seen Erminia Aglietti. But usually it would come upon me in the late
afternoon, at the onset of those beautiful, wearisome
summer evenings. I would walk down to the lake, untie
one of the boats, and row until I was tired and hot, but
then I would find it impossible to return home. Into a
tavern then or a beer-garden. There I sampled various
wines, and drank and brooded. The next day I occasionally felt half sick. A dozen times I was overcome by
such ghastly misery and self-disgust that I resolved to
stop drinking altogether. Yet then I would go out and
drink again and again. Gradually, as I learned to distinguish among the wines and their effects, I began to
enjoy them with a genuine awareness. Finally I decided
in favor of the dark-red Veltliner. The first glass tasted
harsh and provocative, but then it clouded my
thoughts, so that they became calm and dreamy; as I
continued to drink, it cast its spell over me and began to
compose poems as if by itself. Then I would behold
myself surrounded by all the landscapes I had ever
loved, bathed in a delicious light, and I could see myself
wandering through them, singing, dreaming. Then I
sensed life coursing through me. This whole experience
resolved itself into comfortable melancholy, as though
I heard folksongs played on a violin, and knew of some
fortune somewhere that I had been close to and that
had passed me by.

It so happened that I gradually drank less often by

myself, and now did so in the company of all sorts of
people. As soon as I was no longer alone, the wine
affected me differently; I became gregarious yet not
exuberant. I felt a strange cool fever. An aspect of my
character suddenly blossomed forth that belonged less
to the species of decorative garden flower than to the
species of thistle or nettle. As I became more eloquent a
sharp, cool spirit would take hold of me, making me
self-assured, superior, critical, and witty. If there were
people whose presence irked me, I quickly began need
ling them—delicately at first, then coarsely and stubbornly until they left. Since childhood, I had never
found people indispensable or had great need of them.
Now I began to regard them with a critical, ironic eye. I
preferred inventing and telling stories in which people's
relationships with one another were represented
satirically or were bitterly mocked. I had no idea how I
came upon this deprecatory tone; it erupted from me
like a long-festering sore and it was to stay with me for
years. If, for a change, I happened to spend an evening
drinking by myself again, I would again dream of
mountains, stars, and melancholy music.

During this time I wrote a number of sketches on
society, culture, and contemporary art, a venomous
little book which was the product of my barroom conversations. My historical studies, which I still pursued
assiduously, provided me with background material
that I used as a kind of underpinning for my satires.

This book helped me become a regular contributor to one of the larger newspapers, and I now had almost enough money to live on. These sketches soon afterward were published in book form and were even quite successful. I now abandoned philology altogether. I had reached the upper echelons; connections with German periodicals were forged as a matter of course and raised me from my previous obscurity and impoverishment into the circle of recognized authors. I was earning my living; I relinquished scholarship. I was sailing rapidly toward the despicable life of a professional man of letters.

Despite my success and my vanity, despite my satires and my unrequited love, the warm glow of youth—its lightheartedness and sadness—still enveloped me. Despite my gift for irony and a harmless touch of the supercilious, I had not lost sight of the goal of my dreams—some great fortune, a completion of myself. I had no idea what form it would take. I only felt that life would have to toss some very special luck at my feet— perhaps it would be fame or love, perhaps a satisfaction of my longing and an elevation of my being. I was like a page who dreams of noble ladies, accolades, and princely honors.

I thought I was on the verge of some momentous happening. I did not know that everything I had so far experienced was mere chance, that my life still lacked a deep individual melody of its own. I did not know yet that I suffered from a longing which neither love nor fame can satisfy. Therefore I enjoyed my slight and somewhat questionable success with all the exuberance I could command. It felt good to be in the company of intelligent people and to see their faces turn eagerly and attentively to me when I spoke.

At times I was struck by the fervor with which these souls longed for some form of redemption. Yet what strange paths they were taking toward that goal. Though belief in God was considered foolish, almost in bad taste, people believed in names like Schopenhauer, Buddha, Zarathustra, and many others. There were young unknown poets who performed solemn rites before statues and paintings in fashionably furnished apartments. They would have been ashamed to do so before God, but they knelt down before the Zeus of Otricoli. There were miserably dressed ascetics who tortured themselves with abstinence: their god's name was either Buddha or Tolstoy. There were artists who, by resorting to wallpaper in carefully selected color schemes, to music, food, wines, perfumes, or cigars, induced states of extraordinary and unusual excitement in themselves. They discoursed easily and with affected naturalness about musical lines, color congruences, and similar matters and were always looking for the "personal" touch, which generally consisted of some small, harmless self-deception or quirk. Though I found this spectacle amusing and ridiculous, I sensed how much deep-felt longing and genuine passion flared up and was consumed thus.

Of all the fantastically dressed, fashionable poets, artists, and philosophers whose acquaintance I made during that time, I cannot think of one who has accomplished anything noteworthy. Among them there was a north German my age, a pleasant little fellow, a delicate and dear person who was sensitive to everything artistic. He was considered one of the great poets of the future, and I remember listening to him recite his poems, which possessed an exceptionally fragrant, soulful quality. He was the only one of us who might have become a real poet. Later I heard by chance what happened to him: having been intimidated by bad reviews of one of his books, the hypersensitive poet withdrew altogether and fell into the hands of a patron who, instead of spurring him on, brought about his complete ruin in a short time. He lived a vapid aesthete's existence at his patron's villa with that man's nervous ladies and began to think of himself as a misunderstood hero; sadly misled, he went about destroying his reason systematically with pre-Raphaelite ecstasies and Chopin's music.

I realized the danger of frequenting this circle and later came to think of this fledgling crew of eccentrically dressed poets and beautiful souls with nothing but horror and pity. Well, my peasant nature luckily kept me from falling prey to this circus.

Nobler and more rewarding than fame, wine, love, and wisdom was friendship. It alone stirred me out of my inborn sluggishness and kept my youth unspoiled and as fresh as the dawn. Even today I know of nothing more delicious than an honest and forthright friendship between two men, and if something like homesickness for my youth overcomes me during periods of reflection, I think back upon nothing with as much longing as my student friendships.

Since my infatuation with Erminia, I had neglected Richard. I did not even notice it at first, but after a few weeks I began to feel guilty. I confessed everything to him; he told me that he had seen misfortune coming and pitied me. I renewed our bonds as unreservedly and enviously as ever. What ease and agility in dealing with people and life I acquired during that time I owe entirely to him. He was handsome and glad in body and soul, and life did not seem to have a darker side for him. Though he was intelligent and worldly enough to be aware of the passions and confusions of our time, they passed over him without injuring him. His walk, his speech, in fact his entire being, were supple, light-hearted, and immensely likable.

However, he showed little appreciation of my liking for wine. He would join me occasionally, but for the most part he had had his fill after two glasses and regarded my far greater consumption with naïve astonishment. But when he noticed that I was suffering or about to succumb to a fit of melancholy, he would play music for me, read to me, or take me on walks. During these small expeditions we were often as high-spirited as little boys. Once, I remember, we lay in a wooded valley at noontime, threw pine cones at each other, and sang irreverent verses to pious tunes. The clear swift stream splashed so cool and inviting that at length we undressed and lay down in the cold water. Then it occurred to Richard to do a pantomime. He sat down on a mossy rock and played the Lorelei, while I drifted past him like the boatman in his ship. He looked so girlishly demure and made such faces that I, who was to affect the deepest woe, had all I could do to contain my laughter. Suddenly we heard voices. A group of tourists appeared on the footpath and we had to hide our nakedness quickly under a mound that jutted out over the stream. As the blissfully ignorant troupe passed us, Richard emitted a series of highly peculiar noises, grunting, squeaking, and hissing in turn. The people stopped dead in their tracks, turned around, peered into the water, and were on the point of discovering us when Richard popped out of his hiding place, looked at the indignant troupe, and intoned with a deep voice and priestly gesture: "Go your way in peace." He ducked away immediately, pinched my arm, and said: "That was an imitation too."

"An imitation of what?"

"Pan frightens the herdsmen," he answered, laughing. "Unfortunately there were a few women among them."

Though he took little notice of my historical studies, he soon shared my infatuation with St. Francis of Assisi. But he would make an occasional crack even about him, which would make me furious. We imagined the blessed sufferer wandering through the Umbrian landscape, enthusiastic, like a big lovable child, rejoicing in God and filled with humble love of all mankind. Together we read his immortal hymn to the sun and knew it almost by heart. Once, as we were returning from a steamboat excursion across the lake, the evening breeze ruffling the golden water, Richard asked softly: "How does our saint put it?"

And I quoted: *"Laudato si, misignore, per frate vento e per aere e nubilo e sereno et omne tempo!"*

When we quarreled or insulted each other, it always ended with Richard hurling such a profusion of amusing nicknames at me that I was soon forced to laugh and my anger lost its sting. The only time my friend was even a little serious was when he played or listened to a piece by one of his favorite composers. Yet even such an event he would interrupt with a joke. Still, his love of art was a pure and heartfelt devotion and his feeling for what was genuine and important seemed to me infallible.

He had a wonderful knack for the delicate and fine art of consoling, of sympathetic sharing and easing of sorrow when one of his friends was in distress. If he happened to find me in ill humor, he would amuse me with innumerable anecdotes and his voice then had a calming and cheering quality that I was able to resist only rarely.

Richard showed a certain respect for me because I was more serious than he; yet, my physique impressed him far more. He boasted about it in front of friends and was proud to have a friend who could have strangled him with one hand. He set great store in physical prowess and agility; he taught me tennis, rowed and swam with me, took me horseback riding, and was not satisfied until I played billiards as skillfully as he. It was his favorite game, and he played it not only masterfully but with artistry, and was always particularly lively and witty at it.

His opinion of my writing did not exceed my own. He once said to me: "Look, I always thought you were a poet and I still think you are, not because you write for the literary journals but because there is something beautiful and deep alive in you that will break out sooner or later. *That* will be genuine poetry."

Meanwhile, the weeks slipped like thin coins through our fingers, and the time was quite unexpectedly at hand when Richard had to think about returning home. With slightly feigned high spirits we enjoyed the waning weeks and finally agreed that some festive undertaking would have to precede our bitter leave-taking, so that it would end on a cheerful and promising note. I suggested a holiday in the Bernese Alps. Yet it was only the beginning of spring, much too early for the Alps. While I racked my brain for other suggestions, Richard wrote his father, quietly preparing a great surprise for me. One day he appeared with a formidable check and invited me to accompany him as a guide through northern Italy.

A dream I had harbored since youth was about to come true. Feverishly I made my small preparations, quickly taught my friend a few words of Italian, and was apprenhensive to the last minute before our departure lest our plans come to nothing.

Our bags were sent ahead, we sat in a train carriage, the green fields and hills flitted past, Lake Urner, the Saint Gotthard pass, then the mountain hamlets and brooks and boulder-strewn slopes and snow-capped peaks of the Ticino, and then the first dark stone houses on the more gently sloped vineyards, and the journey full of expectation along the lakes and through the fertile plains of Lombardy toward the lively, noisy, strangely attractive yet repulsive Milan.

Richard had never tried to imagine what the Cathe-

dral of Milan might look like; he had only heard it mentioned as an architectural masterpiece. So it was a
delightful experience to watch his outraged disappointment. Once he had overcome the initial shock and regained his sense of humor, he was the first to suggest
that we climb to the roof and make our way among the
confused array of gargoyles. We noted with some satisfaction that the hundreds of statues of saints on the
small Gothic spires were of little consequence, at least
the more recent ones, which seemed to have been mass-
produced. For almost two hours we lay on our backs on
the sloping marble slabs, which had been warmed by
the April sun. Contentedly, Richard confessed: "You
know, I wouldn't really mind being disappointed again
the way I was here. During the entire trip I have been a
little afraid that all the treasures we would see would
overwhelm us. And now the whole thing has had such
a human and slightly ridiculous beginning." Then the
confused assemblage of stone figures in whose midst
we were camping aroused the baroque streak in his
imagination.

"Presumably," he said, "the most distinguished and
highest of the saints has his place right up there on the
choir tower. But because it cannot be an altogether delightful experience to balance like an acrobat of stone
on this sharp little pinnacle for all time, it is only fair
that the topmost saint be relieved periodically and

(91

moved up into heaven. Now just imagine what a spectacle ensues when this happens, for all the other saints have to move up one place according to their rank in the hierarchy, each one having to leap onto his predecessor's perch, each one in a great rush and each jealous of those who precede him."

Whenever I visited Milan thereafter, I would remember that afternoon and with a melancholy smile envision the hundreds of marble saints performing their bold leaps.

Genoa, too, provided a rich reward. Shortly after noon on a bright windy day, my arms resting on a broad parapet, my back to the brightly colored city, I beheld for the first time the swell of the great blue flood, the sea. Tossing darkly with unfathomable yearning, eternal and immutable, it hurled itself toward me and I sensed something within me fashioning a friendship for life and in death with this foam-flecked surge.

The unlimited spaciousness of the horizon affected me as deeply. Once again, as in childhood, I beheld the soft blue of immeasurable distances beckoning to me like an open gate. And the feeling swept over me that I was not born for a normal life at home among my people or in cities and houses, but my fate was to wander through foreign regions and make odysseys on the sea. Darkly, the old melancholy longing rose up in me to throw myself on God's mercy and merge my own pitifully insignificant life with the infinite and timeless.

Near Rapallo I went swimming. For the first time I wrestled with waves, tasted the salty tang and experienced the might of the ocean. Around me nothing but clear blue waves, brown-yellow rocks along the shore, a deep calm sky, and the eternal great roar of the sea. The sight of ships passing along the horizon affected me anew each time: black masts and polished white sails, or the small ribbon of smoke from a steamship far away. Next to my favorites, the clouds, I know of nothing more beautiful than a ship sailing at a great distance, growing smaller and smaller, disappearing finally into the horizon.

Then we reached Florence. The city displayed itself to our eyes as I remembered it from hundreds of pictures and a thousand premonitions—sunlit, spacious, hospitable, traversed by a green stream with many bridges, and girdled by sharply outlined hills. The bold tower of the Palazzo Vecchio pointed defiantly into the clear sky. Behind it, at the same height, lay beautiful Fiesole, white and sun-drenched, and all the hills were white and rose-red with the bloom of the fruit trees. The carefree, harmless life of Tuscany opened itself to me like a miracle and soon I felt more at home there than I ever had anywhere else. We idled away our days in churches, piazzas, in little side streets, loggias, and marketplaces; in the evenings we lolled dreamily in gardens on the hillsides, where the lemons were already ripening, or in simple taverns that served Chianti,

(93

where we drank and talked. In between we spent richly rewarding hours in the galleries and in the Bargello, in cloisters, libraries, and sacristies; afternoons in Fiesole, San Miniato, Settignano, Prato.

As we had previously agreed, I would now leave Richard for a week by himself, and I had the noblest and most delicious experience of my youth: wandering through the rich green Umbrian hills. I trod the streets St. Francis had walked, and often felt as though he were walking beside me, full of unfathomable love, joyously and thankfully greeting each bird and mountain spring. I picked lemons and ate them on hills glistening with sunlight, spent my nights in little villages, sang and composed poems within myself, and celebrated Easter in Assisi, in the church of my saint.

I still feel that those eight days I wandered through Umbria were the crown and sunset of my youth. Each day new sources welled up within me and I gazed onto the clear and festive landscape as into the benign eyes of God.

In Umbria I had devotedly traced the steps of St. Francis, the musician of God; in Florence I had savored the illusion of living in the quattrocento. Though I had written satires on contemporary life, I did not realize the ridiculous shabbiness of modern culture until I set foot in Florence. In Florence I began to sense that I would be a stranger in society for the rest of my life, and the desire was born in me to lead my life outside this society, preferably in the south. I did not feel a stranger among people here, and the ease and naturalness of life overjoyed me, especially since the tradition of classical culture and history ennobled and refined it.

The beautiful weeks slipped by in a marvelous series of joyous experiences; never had I seen Richard so enraptured. In our wanderings we came upon out-of-the-way mountain villages basking in the sun, made friends with innkeepers, monks, country girls, and humble village priests; listened to naïve village serenades, fed pretty, brown-skinned children bread and fruit, and gazed down on the glistening Ligurian sea from the sunlit Tuscan hills. Both of us, certain that we were worthy of our good fortune, looked forward to a rich new life. Work, struggle, pleasure, and fame lay within our reach, so we enjoyed our days with no sense of urgency. Even our imminent separation seemed inconsequential; for we knew with greater certainty than ever before that we needed each other and could count on each other for the rest of our lives.

That is the story of my youth. Upon reflection, it seems as brief as a summer night. A little music, love, and vainglory—yet it was beautiful and rich and colorful like an Eleusian feast.

And it was snuffed out as quickly and pathetically as a candle in the wind.

Richard took leave of me in Zurich. I never saw him

again. Two weeks later he drowned while bathing in a
ridiculously small river in southern Germany. I did not
attend the funeral, for I learned of his death a few days
after he was buried. Then I threw myself on the floor of
my little room blaspheming God and life with horrible,
vile curses, cried, and went mad. I had not realized
until then that my friendship was my sole possession.
Now it was gone.

I could not bear to stay in a town where each step I
took filled me with a host of memories that seemed to
choke me. It was all the same to me what happened
now; I was sick to the core of my soul and had a dread
of everything alive. And I had few expectations that my
harrowed being would right itself and drive coura-
geously with newly hoisted sails into a time of manhood
that promised to be even harsher. God had decreed that
I was to offer the best part of myself to a pure and
joyous friendship. Like two swiftly moving skiffs, we
had stormed forward together, and Richard's skiff was
the colorful, fragile, happy, and loved one, to which my
eye clung and which I trusted to bear me along toward
beautiful destinies. Now it had sunk with no more than
a brief cry, leaving me rudderless and adrift on waters
that had suddenly darkened.

It would be my task now to withstand this hard test
and, setting my course by the stars, to set out on a new
journey for the crown of life—with the chance of

losing my way once more. I had believed in friendship, in the love of women, and in youth. Now that one after the other had left me, why did I not put my trust in God? But all my life I have been as timid and obstinate as a child, always confident that real life would come like a storm and overwhelm me. It would make me wise and rich, then bear me on its huge wings toward a ripe fortune.

Wise and frugal, life remained silent, however, and let me drift. It sent me neither storms nor stars but waited so that I would become aware of my insignificance again and in patience lose my obstinacy. It let me perform my little comedy of pride and knowledge, ignoring this as it waited for the lost child to find his way back to his mother.

Chapter Five

I NOW COME to a period in my life apparently more lively and colorful than earlier periods, one which would provide me with the material for a slight but fashionable novel. I could tell how I became the editor of a German newspaper, how I allowed too great a freedom to my pen and malicious tongue and suffered the consequences; how I became a notorious drinker, finally resigned my position after much unpleasantness, and managed to have myself assigned to Paris as a special correspondent; how I lived wildly, wasting my time in that corrupt place, and got involved in all kinds of scrapes.

If I skip this interlude and deprive those of my readers with a taste for the sordid of the intimate details, it isn't because I'm afraid. I admit I entered one dead-end street after the other, saw all sorts of vile things, and became involved in them. The attraction of *la vie bohème* lost all its appeal and you must allow me to concentrate on what is pure and good and leave those wasted, rejected years behind me.

One evening as I sat in the Bois de Boulogne, wondering whether to have done with Paris or even with

life itself, I reviewed my entire existence for the first
time in years and reached the conclusion that I had
little to lose by suicide.

All at once I imagined that day long since past—an
early summer morning in the mountains as I knelt at
the side of the bed on which my mother lay dying. Not
having been able to think of that morning for so long
startled me with shame and the stupid impulse to
commit suicide disappeared. For I believe that no one,
unless foolish or mad, is capable of taking his own life
if he has witnessed the end of another person's good
life. Once again I saw my mother dying, watched the
sober labor of death on her face, ennobling it. Death appeared harsh yet as strong and as kind as a father who
fetches a lost child.

Now I realized that death is our wise and good
brother who knows the right hour and on whom we can
depend. I began to understand that suffering and dis-
appointments and melancholy are there not to vex us or
cheapen us or deprive us of our dignity but to mature
and transfigure us.

A week later my trunks were packed and on their way
to Basel. I set off on foot, covering large stretches of
southern France; with each day I walked, my ungodly
Paris period, pursuing me in memory like a stench,
turned more and more into a fog and blew away. I
followed a *cour d'amour,* spent my nights in castles,

mills, or barns, and drank southern wines in the company of dark and loquacious country folk.

Unkempt, lean, sunburned, and inwardly changed I arrived in Basel two months later. This was my first great trip on foot, the first of many. For there are few places between Locarno and Verona, between Basel and Brig, Florence and Perugia, that my dusty boots have not traversed twice or three times—in pursuit of dreams, none of which has yet been fulfilled.

In Basel I rented a run-down apartment outside town, unpacked my things, and set to work. I was glad I lived in a quiet town where no one knew who I was. I had kept up my connections with some newspapers and journals and had sufficient work to keep me alive. The first few weeks were good, but gradually my melancholy returned, staying with me for days and weeks on end, and would not leave even when I worked. Those who have never felt this melancholy will not understand what I mean. How should I describe it? I was enveloped by a sensation of ghastly loneliness. Between myself and people and life in the city, plazas, houses, and streets, a wide cleavage existed at all times. There would be an accident, newspaper headlines—none of it mattered to me. There were fetes, funerals, fairs, concerts—to what purpose? Why? I ran out of my room, roamed forests, mountains, and highways. The meadows, trees, and fields were silent. They looked at me with mute entreaty, sought to communicate, to be obliging, to greet me. But they stood there unable to say anything, while I understood their suffering and suffered with them because I could not redeem them.

I went to see a doctor, brought a record of my ailments, and tried to describe my suffering to him. He read my notes, questioned me, and then examined me.

"I envy you your good health," he said. "There's nothing wrong with you physically. Try to cheer yourself up with books and music."

"I read new books every day. It happens to be part of my job."

"In any case, you ought to get out in the open more often."

"I take three- or four-hour walks each day, and when I'm on holiday I walk twice that much."

"Then you should force yourself to be with other people. You're in danger of becoming a recluse."

"What does that matter?"

"It matters a great deal. The less you tend to seek out other people, the more you should force yourself to. Your condition can't yet be diagnosed as an illness. It does not seem serious to me, but if you don't lead a more active social life, you might lose your equilibrium one of these days."

The doctor was a sympathetic, well-intentioned man. He felt sorry for me. He introduced me to a scholar whose house was the center of many gatherings and of a certain literary and intellectual life. I went there. People knew.my name, they were friendly, almost kind, and I began to frequent the house.

Once I went on a cold evening in late fall. A young historian and a slim, dark-haired girl were there; no one else. The girl served tea, did the talking, and was snide toward the historian. Afterward she played the piano. Then she told me she had read my satirical pieces but had not enjoyed them. She seemed clever, too clever, and I soon went home.

Eventually people found out that I spent much of my time in bars, that actually I was a drunkard. It hardly surprised me that they should have made this discovery, for rumors flourish readily in academic circles. Yet this shameful piece of information had no untoward effect on my visits. In fact it made me more desirable, for temperance happened to be the rage and most of the ladies and gentlemen belonged to one of several temperance societies. They rejoiced over each sinner who fell into their clutches. One day, the first polite attack was launched against my habit. The disgrace of frequenting bars, the curse of alcoholism—all this viewed from the hygienic, ethical, and social standpoint—were impressed on me in no uncertain terms and I was asked to attend one of the temperance-society evenings. I was startled. I had only a faint notion of the existence of these clubs and their endeavors. The meeting, with its music and religious overtones, struck me as painfully comic and I made no attempt to conceal my feelings. For weeks afterward I was importuned—in the friendliest possible manner, to be sure—until the subject began to bore me. One evening, when the same routine started all over again—all of them sincerely hoping for my conversion—I got desperate and insisted that they spare me this gibberish from now on. The dark, slim girl was present, listened attentively to me, and applauded at the end. But I was too annoyed to pay attention to her.

Once I was delighted to witness a slightly humorous incident that followed an important temperance rally. The society members and guests had dined at headquarters; there were speeches, friendships were struck up, hymns were sung, and the progress of the great cause was celebrated with much hue and cry, but one of the ushers who served as banner-bearer found the alcohol-free speeches too tedious and sneaked off to a nearby tavern. When the solemn demonstration started through the streets, the reprobates lining the sidewalks had a delightful spectacle to jeer at: a gaily inebriated leader at the head of the enthusiastic assemblage, the flag with the blue cross swaying in his arms like the mast of a foundering ship.

Though the drunken usher was whisked away, the

mass of petty vanities, jealousies, and intrigues flourishing between the various competing clubs and commissions remained. The movement split. A few overly ambitious members claimed all credit for themselves and would loudly curse every drunken reprobate not reclaimed in their name. Many noble and selfless coworkers were callously exploited, and those with an inside view of these affairs saw how easily human frailties could thrive under the cover of idealism. I heard about these incidents through secondhand sources and derived a quiet satisfaction from them. On many occasions, returning from one of my nightly bouts, I told myself that, wild as we were, we drunkards were better and more honest persons than the reformers.

In my little room with its unhampered view of the Rhine, I studied and pondered at great length. I was disconsolate that life seemed to pass me by, that no strong current took hold of me, no great passion inflamed me or pulled me out of this stupefying trance. Besides my regular work, I was preparing a book on the lives of the early Minorites, yet this was not creative work but a patient and modest assembling of information. It did not satisfy my longing.

Reflecting on the time I had spent in Zurich and Paris, I tried to clarify for myself the real desires, passions, and ideals of my contemporaries. One of them had set himself the task of persuading people to discard outmoded furniture, wallpaper, and fashions, introducing them to freer and more beautiful surroundings; another devoted his efforts to popularizing Haeckel's monism. Others strove for universal peace. Still another acquaintance was fighting for the impoverished lower classes, and another collected funds and lectured in behalf of building theaters and museums for the public. And here in Basel people combated alcoholism.

All these endeavors were imbued with vigor and movement; yet none of them mattered to me. It would have made no difference to me or the kind of life I led if any or all of these objectives had been achieved. Unhappy, I sank back into my chair, pushed papers and books away, and reflected. I could hear the Rhine surging past and the wind rustling. I listened intently to this great melancholy language that seemed to suffuse everything with sadness and longing. I saw pale clouds swoop like frightened birds through the night sky, heard the Rhine coursing, and thought of my mother's death, of St. Francis, of my homeland and the snow-capped mountains, and of my friend Richard, who had drowned. I saw myself scaling precipices to pick "Alpine roses" for Rösi Girtanner, animated by music and conversation in Zurich, rowing with Erminia Aglietti in the evening; I saw myself despairing over Richard's

death, voyaging and returning, convalescing and becoming miserable once more. To what purpose? Why?
Oh, God, had all of it been a mere game, mere chance,
a mirage? Hadn't I struggled and suffered agonies for
friendship and beauty and truth? Did not the wave of
longing and love still well up fiercely within me?

Then I would be all set to go out and drink. I blew
out my lamp, groped my way down the steep, winding
staircase, and went into one of the wine-halls. Being a
steady customer, I was received with respect, though I
was usually cantankerous and sometimes unspeakably
rude. I read the satirical magazine *Simplicissimus,*
which never failed to infuriate me, drank my wine, and
waited for it to soothe me. When the kind god touched
me with his gentle hands, my limbs would become
pleasantly weary and my soul would enter the land of
dreams.

At times it surprised me that I treated people so
boorishly and derived pleasure from snapping at them.
The waitresses at wine-halls I frequented feared me
and cursed me as a roughneck for always finding fault
with them. When I happened to enter into conversation
with the other guests, I was rude or mocked them, and
naturally they replied in kind. Still, I managed to latch
on to several drinking companions, all of them aging,
incurable alcoholics. We spent some evenings on fairly
tolerable terms. Among them was an old ruffian, de-

signer by trade, a misogynist and foul-mouthed drunk
of the first order. If I happened on him in some tavern,
a night-long bout of drinking invariably ensued. We
would start by bantering jokes back and forth, slowly
finishing our first bottle of red wine. Drinking as such
gradually began to predominate, and the conversation
petered out. We sat facing each other, quietly drawing
on our cigars, emptying our respective bottles. We were
evenly matched, refilled our bottles at the same time,
and watched each other drink, half respectfully, half
with malicious glee. At grape-harvest time in the late
fall we once hiked through some vine-growing villages
in the Markgräferland and at the Stag in Kirchen the
old buzzard told me his life's story. I only remember
that it was interesting and unusual; I've forgotten all
the details.

One thing I do remember is his description of a
drinking bout in the later part of his life. He was out in
the country somewhere at a village festival, and being
seated at the table of honor, he toasted the pastor and
mayor so often that they became drunk very quickly.
The pastor, however, had to give a speech. After much
effort was exerted to maneuver him onto the platform,
he made a number of outrageous statements and was
bundled off in disgrace, whereupon the mayor tried to
fill the breach. He held forth in a bold and impressive
manner at first, but the suddenness of the event had

made him unwell and his impromptu speech ended in an unusual and indelicate manner.

I would gladly have heard this story and others repeated by my drinking companion, but as a result of a quarrel at a shooting match, we became irreconcilable enemies. Now both of us sat in the same tavern, each at his own table, as enemies. But out of habit we watched each other, drank at the same rate, and sat there until, the last guests, we were finally asked to move on. We were never friends again.

The interminable probing of the causes of my melancholy and my inability to cope with life was fruitless and wearying. Still I did not feel worn out or exhausted but full of dark urges, convinced that I would yet succeed in creating something deep and good, in snatching a bit of luck from life. But would this lucky moment ever come? I thought with bitterness of those high-strung modern artists who drove themselves to the pitch of artistic creation with the help of artificial stimulants, whereas I allowed my resources to lie untapped within me. I tried to analyze what kind of block or demon was constraining my soul within this vigorous body. Too, I was possessed by the notion that I was someone unusual, someone whom life had mistreated and whose suffering was unknown to anyone, who was misunderstood.

The diabolical thing about melancholy is not that it

makes you ill but that it makes you conceited and shortsighted; yes, almost arrogant. You lapse into bad taste, thinking of yourself as Heine's Atlas, whose shoulders support all the world's puzzles and agonies, as if thousands, lost in the same maze, did not endure the same agonies. In my state of isolation and estrangement I too failed to realize that the traits and peculiarities of character I took to be exclusively mine were in fact part of my family's heritage, my family's affliction, and proper to all Camenzinds.

Every few weeks I would drop in at the home of my hospitable scholar friend. Gradually I became acquainted with most of the people who went there; there were many young academicians, quite a few of them German, who worked in a wide variety of fields; a few painters and musicians, as well as some ordinary citizens, who brought their wives. Often I would gaze at these people with a kind of astonishment. I knew that they saw one another several times a week, and I did not understand how they could have anything left to say to each other. The majority of them were stereotyped examples of *homo socialis* and all of them seemed to have some affinity with one another, sharing a gregariousness and superficiality that I alone lacked. Among them were quite a few fine and distinguished people whose vigor and presence of mind seemed to be not at all, or only slightly, diminished by this constant socializing. I was only able to talk to one person. at a time. Rushing from one to the other, stopping only for a brief moment, making a stab at complimenting one of the ladies while attending to a cup of tea, two conversations, and the piano playing, all at one and the same time, with a look of animated amusement—that I could not do. Worst of all was when I was forced to speak about literature and art. I observed that precious little thought was given to these subjects and that they only provided occasion for much lying and gabbing.

I lied along as well as I could, but it gave me no pleasure and I found this chitchat boring and humiliating. I much preferred to listen to a woman talking about her children or to tell about my trips or little things that had happened to me during the day or to talk about actual events. At these moments I could be almost friendly and glad. After one of these evenings, however, I usually stopped by a wine-hall and slaked my parched throat, drowning my unspeakable boredom in draughts of wine.

At one of these gatherings I saw the dark-haired girl again. There were many people present; there was music, and the chatter grew as loud and insufferable as usual. I was sitting in an out-of-the-way corner with a portfolio of sketches of Tuscany on my knees. These were not the usual hackneyed little sketches of the obvious sights; they were more intimate: landscapes sketched by traveling companions and friends who had given them to my host. I even discovered among them a drawing of a small stone house with narrow windows in the isolated valley of San Clemente, a house I recognized because I had taken many walks in that region. The valley lies close to Fiesole, but most tourists never set foot there because it is virtually devoid of antiquities. It is a valley of severe yet remarkable beauty, arid and almost uninhabited, hemmed in by stark, bare mountains; remote, melancholy, pristine.

The girl stepped up to me and looked over my shoulder.

"Why do you spend so much time by yourself, Herr Camenzind?"

I was annoyed. She feels neglected by the other men, I thought, and now she comes to me.

"Well, won't you give me an answer?"

"Excuse me. But what am I supposed to answer? I sit by myself because that's the way I like it."

"Am I disturbing you then?"

"You're amusing."

"Thanks, the feeling is mutual." And she sat down. I made no attempt to put the portfolio away.

"You're from the mountain country, aren't you?" she asked. "I wonder if you could describe it to me. My brother tells me no one but Camenzinds live in your village. Is that true?"

"Practically," I muttered. "There's Füssli the baker, and there's an innkeeper by the name of Nydegger."

"And the rest are all Camenzinds? Are they all related?"

"More or less."

I handed her a sketch. She held the sheet in such a way that I saw she knew how something like that should be handled, and I told her as much.

"You praise me, but like a teacher." She laughed.

"Don't you want to look at the sketch?" I asked brusquely. "If not, I can put it back with the others."

"What is it of?"

"San Clemente."

"Where?"

"Near Fiesole."

"Have you been there?"

"Yes, a few times."

"What does the valley look like? This doesn't give you much of an idea."

I thought for a moment. The stark yet beautiful landscape came into view and I half closed my eyes to hold on to the image. It was a little while before I spoke again, and I was pleased that she had not interrupted me. She seemed to realize that I was meditating.

Then I described San Clemente as it lies parched and immense, bearing the brunt of the sun on a summer afternoon. In nearby Fiesole there is industry; people weave straw hats and baskets, or hawk souvenirs and oranges, or cheat tourists or beg from them. Florence, where the old and the new mingle, lies even farther down the valley. But Fiesole and Florence are out of sight of San Clemente. No painter has worked there, no Roman monument was erected there; human history passed this desolate valley by. Only the sun and rain do battle with the earth there, crooked pine trees maintain a precarious existence, and with their lean tops the few cypresses feel the air for oncoming storms that will cut short the miserable lives to which their parched roots cling. Occasionally an oxcart from a neighboring dairy farm will come by, or a farmer and his family will wander past on their way to Fiesole, but these are chance visitors, and the red skirts the farm women wear, which seem so smartly gay elsewhere, are out of place in San Clemente, so you don't mind leaving them out of the picture.

I told her how I had hiked through the valley with a friend, had rested at the feet of cypress trees and leaned against their slender trunks; and how the sad and beautiful magic of the strange, lonely valley had reminded me of the valleys at home.

Then we were both silent.

"You are a poet," said the girl after a moment.

I made a face.

"I don't mean it that way," she went on. "Not because

you write stories, but because you understand and love nature. It doesn't matter to most people that the wind sings in the trees or that a mountain shimmers in the sunlight. But you find life in all this, a life you can partake of."

I replied that no one understood nature and that all searching and all desire to comprehend really complicated matters more and made one melancholy. A tree bathed in sunlight, a weathered stone, an animal, a mountain, each has life, has a tale to tell, is alive, suffers, endures, experiences joy, dies—but we don't understand it.

As I talked, soothed by her patience and attentiveness, I looked at her more closely. Her gaze was fixed on my face, her expression calm and rapt with interest as though she were a child—or, rather, like an adult who forgets himself entirely while listening and whose eyes, unselfconsciously, again become those of a child. And as I observed her, little by little I realized, with the naïve joy of revelation, that she was very beautiful.

When I ceased speaking, she too was silent. Then, as if startled by something, she squinted into the lamplight.

"I don't know your name, you know," I said suddenly.

"Elizabeth."

She left me and soon afterwards was asked to play the piano. She played well. But when I joined the group at the piano I noticed she was no longer quite as beautiful.

As I walked down the comfortably old-fashioned staircase, I overheard a snatch of conversation between two painters who were putting on their coats in the hall.

"At least he had a good time flirting with Elizabeth," one of them said, laughing.

"Still waters . . ." said the other. "He didn't pick the worst one either."

So those fools were already gabbing. It occurred to me that I had confided the most intimate thoughts and a good portion of my memories to this young girl, confided in her almost against my will. What had made me do it? And they were already talking, the bastards.

I went away and avoided the house for several months. By chance, one of those two painters was the first to broach the subject when I met him in the street.

"Why aren't you coming to the house any more?"

"Because I'm sick of their damned gossip!"

"Oh, yes, those women!" he laughed.

"No," I retorted. "I mean the men, our artist friends in particular."

During these months I saw Elizabeth only a few times on the street, once in a shop and once in the art museum. Usually she looked pretty, never beautiful. There was something unusual about the movement of her overly slim body, which, though generally it suited her, could also seem exaggerated or artificial. But that time in the museum, she was beautiful—beautiful beyond words. She did not notice me sitting on the side leafing through the catalogue; she was standing nearby, completely absorbed in a large Segantini. The painting depicted several farm girls working on sparse meadows, in the background jagged mountains which reminded me of the Stockhorn range, and above it all, in a cool, transparent sky, an exceedingly well-rendered ivory cloud. It made you reel when you set eyes on it: from its knotted, involuted mass you could see that the wind had just packed and kneaded it; the cloud was about to soar and drift away. Elizabeth had grasped this and yielded to it completely. And her soul, usually veiled, once more revealed its inner face, laughed softly out of wide-open eyes, made her small mouth childishly soft, and smoothed out the clever, severe fold between her brows. The beauty and genuineness of a great work of art made her soul display its own beauty and truth.

I sat quietly to the side, contemplating the beautiful Segantini cloud and the lovely girl under its spell. Then I became afraid that she would turn around and want to talk to me and lose her beauty again, so quickly and silently I left the room.

At this time I began again to delight in nature, and my attitude toward it underwent a change. Time and time again I roamed through the magnificent country surrounding the town, mainly into the Jura, which I liked best of all. Whenever I saw these woods, mountains, meadows, and orchards, I sensed that they stood there waiting for something. Perhaps for me, but certainly for love.

And so I began to love all these things. An overpowering longing within me responded to their silent beauty and, within myself as well, there arose the yearning to be conscious, understood, and loved.

Many people say they "love nature," by which they mean they don't dislike the charms nature displays before them. They go on outings, delight in the beauty of the earth as they trample meadows and tear off flowers and sprigs, only to discard them or let them wilt at home. That is how they love nature. This love overcomes them on Sundays when the weather is fine and they are moved by the goodness of their hearts. Actually they have no need for such feelings, for isn't man "the crowning glory of nature"? Yes, of course, the crown!

So I peered more and more greedily into the abyss of things. I listened to the wind sing in the trees, listened to brooks roar through gorges and gentle streams glide through the plains, and I knew these sounds were the language of God: if I understood their dark, archaic, beautiful language, it would be the rediscovery of paradise. Books make little mention of this. It is the Bible that contains the wonderful expression "the groaning and travailing of creation." Yet I felt that men through the ages had been overwhelmed by the ineffable in life, had abandoned their daily tasks and fled into seclusion ·to hearken to the song of creation, to contemplate the fleeting clouds, restlessly and longingly as hermits, penitents, and saints to implore the Eternal.

Have you ever been in Pisa, in the Camposanto? Its walls are covered with the faded frescoes of past centuries, one of them depicting the life of hermits in the Theban desert. Despite its faded colors, the naïve picture exudes such bliss and peace that grief suddenly overwhelms you and you long to weep away your sins and wickedness in some remote and holy place, never to return. Innumerable artists have sought thus to express their homesickness—in marvelous paintings. Any one of Ludwig Richter's affectionate paintings of children sings the same song as the frescoes in Pisa.

Why did Titian, who loved the present and the physical, endow some of his lucidly representational paintings with a background of tenderest blue? Just one brushstroke of warm, deep blue. Whether it manifests distant mountains or limitless space, one cannot tell. Titian the realist did not himself know. He did not do it for reasons of color harmony, as the art historians would have it. It was his tribute to the ineffable, which was deeply alive in the soul of even this happy, light-hearted man. Art, it seemed to me, had sought in all ages to provide a language for the mute longing of the divine within us.

St. Francis expressed this more beautifully and completely, yet in a more childlike way. Only now did I really understand him. By encompassing the love of earth, plants, stars, animals, storms, and seas in his love of God, he superseded the Middle Ages, even Dante, to discover the language of the eternally human. He calls all creation and natural phenomena his dear brothers and sisters. Later in life, when the doctors ordered that he have his forehead seared by a red-hot iron, he greeted the terrible instrument as his "dear brother, the fire," despite his dread of pain.

As I learned to love nature as if it were a person, to listen to it as if to a comrade or traveling companion speaking a foreign tongue, my melancholy, though not cured, was ennobled and cleansed. My eyes and ears were sharpened, I learned to grasp nuances of tone and subtleties of distinction. I longed to put my ear nearer and nearer to the heartbeat of every living thing, so as to understand perhaps, perhaps one day be granted the gift of expressing this heartbeat in poetry which others would awaken to. This pulse would send them to the springs of all rejuvenation and purification. But this was only a fervent wish, a dream . . . I did not know

CHAPTER FIVE

whether it would be fulfilled and concentrated on what was close to hand: I offered my love to every visible thing and set myself to regard nothing with indifference or contempt.

It is impossible to express the revitalizing, soothing effect this had on my somber life. Nothing is nobler or more joyful than an unspoken, constant, dispassionate love, and if I have a heartfelt wish, it is that a few, or even one or two, of my readers be brought to learn this pure and blessed art. Some are born knowing this love and practice it unawares throughout their lives—these are God's favorites, the good children among men. Some learn it at the expense of great suffering, which is evident if you have ever noticed the resolute, quiet, glowing eyes of some cripples or victims of misfortune. If you don't care to listen to me and my poor words, visit those who have overcome and transfigured their suffering through dispassionate love.

I myself am still pitifully far from achieving this state of perfection that I have venerated in many who have suffered. Throughout the years I rarely lacked the consoling belief that I knew the right path. Yet it would be false to say that I never strayed from it, for I rested whenever I could and was not spared many a wrong turn. Two selfish tendencies warred within me against genuine love. I was a drunkard and I was unsociable. Though I cut down considerably on my intake of wine,

I would still surrender completely every few weeks to the guile of the god of the vine leaves. Yet it was only rarely that I would spend the night in some drunken escapade or sprawled out on the street—the god of wine loves me and tempts me to drink only when his spirit and mine enter into friendly dialogue. Nonetheless, I would feel guilty for a long stretch after one of my bouts. But, of all things, I could not give up my love of wine, for I had inherited too strong a bent from my father. For years I had fostered this legacy with care and piety, and made it thoroughly my own. So I helped myself out of this predicament by entering into a half-serious, half-mocking pact. My Franciscan song of praise from now on included "my dear brother, wine."

Chapter Six

ANOTHER WEAKNESS OF MINE was even more troublesome: I disliked people generally, and lived as a recluse, inclined to greet any human touch with mockery or disdain.

When I first resolved to lead a new life I did not give this much thought; it seemed proper to leave other people to fend for themselves and to reserve all my tenderness, devotion, and sympathy for mute nature. At night, before going to bed, I would suddenly remember a hill, the edge of a wood, some favorite solitary tree that I had neglected for a long time. Now it stood in the night wind, dreaming, slumbering perhaps, sighing, its branches trembling. What did it really look like at this very moment? I would leave the house, find the tree, and peer at its indistinct shape in the darkness. I regarded it with astonished tenderness, carrying its dusky image back home with me.

You'll smile. This love may have been mistaken, yet it was not wasted. The only question was how I would find my way from a love of nature to love of mankind.

Well, once you've made a beginning, the rest always follows on its own. The idea of my great poetic creation hovered before my mind's eye; it seemed even more possible than before. And what if my love of nature should enable me to speak the language of woods and streams—for whom would I be doing this? Not solely for those I was fondest of, but really for the sake of a mankind I wanted to lead toward love, even teach to love. Yet with most people I was uncouth, scornful, and unloving. I felt this split within myself and knew I must struggle against unfriendliness. This was difficult because my isolation and personal circumstances made me harsh and mean, especially in social relations. It was not enough to be a little less severe at home or at the tavern, or occasionally to greet a passer-by on the street. Besides, as soon as I tried this I realized how thoroughly my relationships with people had deteriorated: even when my gestures were not hostile, they were greeted with coolness or suspicion—people thought I was mocking them. The worst of it was that for over a year I had avoided the home of the scholar, my only real acquaintance. I realized I would have to call there first if I wanted to have an entree into social life as lived in this town.

It was ironic that the milk of human kindness, which I despised so thoroughly, finally helped me in this endeavor. As soon as I thought of the scholar's house, a picture of Elizabeth came to my mind, as beautiful as she had looked standing before the Segantini cloud. I realized what a large role she had played in my longing and melancholy. For the first time in my life I gave serious thought to marriage. Until now I had been so convinced of my complete unsuitability for married life that I had capitulated to this fact with feelings of caustic self-derision. I was a poet, wanderer, drunkard, lone wolf! Now I felt that my destiny was taking shape as a love match linking me to humanity. It all seemed so tempting and certain! Elizabeth, I had noticed, was receptive to me, and she was a noble person. I remembered how vivid her beauty was when I had told her about San Clemente and when she had stood in front of the Segantini. Over the years I had gathered a great treasure from nature and art which would enable me to reveal to her what was beautiful in all things; I would surround her with everything true and beautiful. Her face and her soul would shed all their sadness and unfold all their potentialities.

Oddly enough, I was completely unaware of the comic aspect of my sudden transformation. I, a recluse who went wholly his own way, overnight had turned into an infatuated fool who dreamed of married bliss and setting up house.

At the first opportunity I called at the house that had always treated me so hospitably, and I was now received with the friendliest of reproaches. I went several times in rapid succession and eventually saw Elizabeth again. Truly, she was beautiful! She looked just as I imagined she would look as my mistress: beautiful and happy. And for a while I just basked in the beauty of her presence. She greeted me in a kindly manner, even affectionately, and with a certain air of intimate friendliness that delighted me.

Do you remember the evening on the lake in the boat, the evening decked out with Japanese lanterns and music, when my declaration of love was nipped in the bud? That had been the pathetic story of a boy in love.

Even more pathetic and sad is the story of Peter Camenzind as a man in love.

Someone mentioned in passing that Elizabeth had just become engaged. I congratulated her, and made the acquaintance of her fiancé when he came to take her home. I congratulated him too. Throughout the evening I wore a smile of benign good will, as irksome to me as a mask. Afterward I did not dash off to the woods or a tavern but sat down on my bed and watched the lamp until it began to smoke and went out. I sat stunned and crushed until finally I came to again. Then grief and despair spread their black wings over me once more and I lay there small and weak and sobbed like a boy.

Whereupon I packed my rucksack, went to the station, and took the morning train home. I felt like climbing mountains again. I wanted to revisit my childhood and find out whether my father was still alive.

We had grown apart. Father's hair had turned completely gray; he no longer carried himself upright and no longer looked very imposing. He treated me shyly, asked no questions, wanted me to take his bed, and seemed embarrassed as well as surprised at my visit. He still owned the little house but had sold the meadows and cattle. He received a small annuity and did a few odd jobs here and there.

After he left the room, I went to the spot where my mother's bed had stood and the past flowed by me like a broad calm stream. No longer an adolescent, I thought how swiftly the years would follow each other from now on and how soon I too would be a bent, gray man, ready to lie down and die a bitter death. In the old, shabby room, almost unchanged since I had lived there as a boy and learned my Latin and witnessed my mother's death, these thoughts seemed so natural they actually calmed me. Gratefully I remembered the abundance of my youth. A stanza of Lorenzo de Medici's that I had learned in Florence came to mind:

> *Quant' è bella giovenezza,*
> *Ma si fugge tuttavia.*
> *Chi vuol esser lieto, sia:*
> *Di doman non c'è certezza.*

Simultaneously I was surprised to find myself bringing memories from Italy, from history, and from the realm of learning into this old and familiar room.

I gave my father some money and in the evening we went to the inn. Everything appeared to be just as it was the last evening we had spent there, except that I paid for the wine. When my father boasted about champagne and described the wine that produced a star-shaped foam, he cited me as his authority and acknowledged that my capacity for drink was now greater than his. I inquired about the wizened peasant over whose bald pate I had poured wine the last time I'd been in the inn, he who had been so full of tricks. I learned he had died long ago and even his jokes had been forgotten. I drank Vaud wine, listened in on the conversations, and told a few stories myself. When I walked home with my father in the moonlight and he continued rambling and gesticulating in his intoxication, I felt a peculiar enchantment I had never felt before. Images from the past pressed upon me—Uncle Konrad, Rösi Girtanner, my mother, Richard, and Erminia. They seemed to me like a picture book whose content surprises you because everything is so beautiful and well made, whereas in reality it was not half so lovely. How fast everything had rushed past me into forgetfulness! Yet it was now engraved clearly and distinctly within me:—half a lifetime that my memory had stored without conscious effort on my part.

Only after we were home and my father finally quieted down and fell asleep did I think of Elizabeth. It had been yesterday that she greeted me and I admired her and congratulated her fiancé. So much seemed to have happened since then—my grief awoke and mingled with the flood of memories to beat against my selfish and ill-protected heart like the Föhn against a trembling and fragile Alpine hut. I could not bear to stay in the house. I climbed out the window, walked to the lake, unfastened the boat, which had been badly neglected, and rowed quietly out into the pale night. The mountains, veiled in silvery mist, kept solemn watch; the moon, which was almost full, seemed to be suspended just above the peak of the Schwarzenstock. It was so quiet I could hear the Sennalpstock waterfall rushing in the distance. The ghosts of my homeland and of my youth touched me with their pale wings, crowded upon me in my small boat, and pointed entreatingly with outstretched hands. They made painful and incomprehensible gestures.

What was the meaning of my life? Why had so many joys and sorrows passed over me? Why had I thirsted for the true and the beautiful and why was my thirst still unquenched? Why had I been in love and suffered so much for these women—I whose head was bowed again in shame for an unfulfilled love. And why had God placed the burning need to be loved in my heart when in fact he had destined me to live the life of a recluse whom no one loved?

The water gurgled dully against the bow and trickled like silver from the oars; the mountains stood close and silent; the cool moonlight shifted from one mist-filled ravine to the other. The ghosts of my youth stood silently about me and gazed at me from deep eyes, silent and searching. It seemed to me I could make out the beautiful Elizabeth among them. She would have loved me and become mine if I had only come at the right time.

I felt it would be best if I were to sink quietly into the pale lake and if no one would ever ask what had become of me. Yet I rowed more swiftly when I noticed the rotten old boat drawing water. Suddenly I felt a chill and hastened to get home.

When I got there, I lay in bed exhausted yet wide awake. I reflected upon my life, seeking to find out what I lacked that would lead me to a happier and more genuine existence. I was well aware that the heart of love is goodness and gladness. I would have to begin to love mankind despite my fresh grief. But how and whom?

Then I thought of my old father and I realized for the first time that I had never loved him as I should have. I had made life difficult for him when I was young; I had gone away and left him alone after my mother's death. I had often been angry with him and finally almost forgotten him completely. The image of him lying on his deathbed began to haunt me: I stood beside it watching his soul slowly ebb away—this soul I had never known and whose love I had never sought to win.

And so I embarked on the difficult yet sweet task of learning from a cantankerous old drunkard instead of from a beautiful and beloved woman. My replies to him became more considerate, I spent as much time with him as I could, read him stories from the almanac, told him about French and Italian wines. I let him continue the little work he had to do, as he would have lost all hold on himself without it. But I never succeeded in getting him to take his measure of wine at home instead of at the inn. We tried it a few times. I fetched wine and cigars and went to some lengths to amuse him at home. The fourth or fifth evening of the experiment, he was silent and stubborn. When I asked what bothered him, he finally complained: "I'm afraid you're never going to let your father set foot in the tavern again."

"Nonsense," I said. "You're my father and it's for you to decide what we'll do."

He looked at me quizzically. Then he picked up his cap and we marched off to the tavern.

It was obvious that my father disliked being alone with me for any length of time, though he did not say so. Besides, I felt the urge to let my wounds heal in a

PETER CAMENZIND

foreign land. "What would you think if I left you again
one of these days?" I asked him. He scratched his head,
shrugged his shoulders, and laughed slyly and expec-
tantly: "As you like." Before leaving, I called on a few
neighbors and on the monks and asked them to keep an
eye on him.

I also reserved one day to climb the Sennalpstock.
From its broad, half-round summit I could look across
mountain ranges and valleys, glistening lakes, and the
haze of distant cities. These sights had filled me with
such powerful longings as a boy. I had gone out to
conquer the beautiful wide world for myself; now it lay
spread out before me as beautiful and enigmatic as
ever. I was ready to go forth and seek my luck once
more.

I had long ago decided that it would benefit my
studies if I were to spend some time in Assisi. First I
returned briefly to Basel, where I took care of a few
pressing matters, packed my few belongings, and sent
them ahead to Perugia. I myself took the train only as
far as Florence and from there hiked south in a leisurely fashion. In this region you do not need to resort
to artifice to get along well with people. The life they
lead is so naïve, open, and free that on your way from
one town to the next you can make as many friends as
you want. I felt safe again and at home. Later on, in
Basel, I knew I would not seek the comfort of human
company in "society" but among the ordinary people.

The mere fact of being alive was a joy in Perugia and Assisi. My interest in historical studies revived, my wounded soul began to heal, and I threw out new bridges to life. My concierge in Assisi, a voluble and devout grocer, entered into a deep friendship with me on the basis of several conversations we had about St. Francis—that was how I acquired the reputation of being a "good Catholic." As undeserved as this honor was, it made it possible for me to become more intimately acquainted with the people; I was no longer suspected of being a heathen, a taint attached to most foreigners in this region. Annunziata Nardini, my concierge, was thirty-four years old, a widow of colossal girth and exquisite manners. On Sundays, attired in cheerful flowery dresses, earrings, a golden chain that dangled on her bosom a collection of hammered-gold medallions tinkling and glistening, she looked the very embodiment of the holiday spirit. She carried about a heavy breviary embossed with silver (whose use, no doubt, would have given her some difficulty) and a beautiful black-and-white rosary with slender silver links (which she could handle much more dexterously). Between church services she would return to her loggetta to hold forth to her awed neighbors on the sins of absent friends. Her round pious face would acquire the poignant expression of a soul at peace with God.

Since my name was too difficult to pronounce correctly, I was simply called Signor Pietro. On golden evenings Signora Nardini and I would sit together in the tiny loggetta, surrounded by neighbors, children, cats, and dogs. In the store itself, amid fruit, baskets of vegetables, seed boxes, and the smoked sausages dangling from the ceiling, we recounted our experiences to each other, discussed harvest prospects; I smoked a cigar, or we both sucked melon slices. I told them about St. Francis, the story of Portiuncula and the saint's church, about St. Clare and the first Franciscan friars. Everyone listened intently, put a thousand questions to me, praised the saint, and gradually entered into a discussion of more recent and more sensational events, with particular preference for stories about robberies and political feuds. Cats, children, and dogs caterwauled around our feet. From personal inclination and to maintain my reputation, I ransacked the saintly legends for edifying and touching anecdotes, and was pleased to have brought along Arnold's *Lives of the Patriarchs and Other Saintly Persons,* among several other books. These frank and simple stories I translated, with little variations, into idiomatic Italian. Passers-by would stop and listen and then join in our talk; in this way, the audience changed three or four times an evening. Signora Nardini and I were the only permanent fixtures and were never absent. I would always have a bottle of red wine beside me, and the frugal

134)

people were impressed by my lordly consumption
Gradually, even the bashful neighborhood girls began
to trust me and take part in the conversations from the
doorstep. They allowed me to make them presents of
small pictures and began to take me for a saint because
I did not tease them with suggestive jokes or seem to
make an effort to gain their confidence. Among them
there were several big-eyed, dreamy beauties who could
have been models for Perugino. I was fond of them all
and enjoyed their playful, good-natured company. Yet I
did not fall in love with any of them, for their beauty
was so much the same that it seemed a racial rather
than a personal quality. Someone else who joined us
was Matteo Spinelli, a young fellow, son of a baker, a
witty and wily joker who could imitate any number of
animals, knew all the latest scandal, and was fairly
bursting with impudent and clever ruses. He would
listen with exemplary piety and humility as I recounted
my legends; then, by naïvely asking a serious or a
malicious question, or by comparing or speculating, he
would ridicule the holy friars, to the dismay of the
grocer's widow and the undisguised delight of most of
the audience.

Frequently I would just sit alone with Signora
Nardini, listen to her edifying discourses, and take an
unholy pleasure in the multitude of her very human
weaknesses. None of her neighbors' faults or vices

escaped her vigilance; to each of them she judiciously assigned an appropriate place in purgatory well in advance. But I had found a place in her heart, and she confided the most trivial experiences and observations to me in great detail and at great length. She inquired how much I paid for every purchase I made, so that I would not be taken advantage of. She had me tell her the lives of the saints, and in return acquainted me with the secrets of the fruit and vegetable trade and the kitchen.

One evening, as we were sitting in the ramshackle loggetta, I sang one of my Swiss songs, to the shrieking delight of the children and girls, and then gave forth with a few brief bursts of yodeling. The children wriggled with pleasure, imitated the sound of the foreign tongue, and showed me how amusingly my Adam's apple jigged up and down when I yodeled. All at once, everybody began speaking of love. The girls giggled, Signora Nardini rolled her eyes imploringly and sighed sentimentally. Finally I was besieged to tell of my own experiences. I made no mention of Elizabeth, but told them about my boat trip with Erminia and my ill-fated proposal of love. It seemed odd to recount this story, of which I had not breathed a word to anyone except Richard, to my inquisitive Umbrian audience in full view of the narrow southern streets and the hills bathed in the golden-red evening light. I told my story without commenting on it as I went along, in the manner of the old novellas, yet my heart was in the telling and I was secretly afraid that my listeners would laugh at me.

But when my tale was told, all eyes looked at me sadly and full of sympathy.

"Such a handsome man," one of the girls exclaimed. "Such a handsome man to be unhappy in love!"

Signora Nardini, however, gently stroked my hair and said: *"Poverino."*

Another girl made me a present of a pear and when I asked her to take the first bite she did so, looking seriously at me. Yet, when I was going to let the others have a bite too, she would not allow it, saying: "No, eat it yourself! I gave it to you because you told us of your bad luck."

"You're bound to fall in love again," said a deeply tanned farmer.

"No," I replied.

"Then you're still in love with this Erminia?"

"Now I only love St. Francis, and he has taught me to love all mankind. You, and all the people of Perugia, and all these children here, and even Erminia's lover."

My idyllic existence became somewhat complicated, even endangered, when I discovered that the good Signora Nardini wished for me to prolong my stay indefinitely by marrying her. This little problem made a

cunning diplomat of me, since destroying her dreams
without ruining our relationship was no easy matter. I
had to think about my return home. If it had not been
for what I hoped to write one day, and an imminent
financial crisis, I would have remained. I might even
have married Signora Nardini thanks to that "financial
crisis." But no, what really made me decide to leave was
my desire to see Elizabeth again—my sorrow had not
healed.

My plump widow acquiesced to the inevitable with
surprising graciousness and did not make me suffer for
her disappointment. My departure, in fact, became
more difficult for me than for her. I was leaving much
more behind than I had ever left before. Never had my
hand been pressed so affectionately by so many people.
They provided me with fruit, wine, cordials, bread, and
sausages for the journey. I had the unusual feeling of
leaving friends to whom it really mattered whether I
went or stayed. Signora Annunziata Nardini kissed me
on both cheeks and her eyes filled with tears.

I used to believe it would be delightful to be loved
without loving back. Now I discovered how painful love
can be when you cannot return it. Still, I felt flattered
that a woman loved me and wanted me for a husband.
Even this touch of vanity meant that I was recover-
ing. I felt sorry for the signora but I would not have
wanted to miss that experience. Gradually I began to

realize how little happiness has to do with the fulfill-
ment of outward wishes. The agonies young men suffer
when they are in love, however painful, have nothing in
common with tragedy. It hurt not to possess Elizabeth,
but my life, my freedom, my work, and my thoughts
were unimpaired, and I could still love her as much as I
wanted from afar. Such thoughts as these and the free
and easy life I had led in Umbria were very good for
me. I had always had an eye for the comic and ridiculous in life, but my ironic turn of mind kept me from
enjoying what I perceived. Now I began to appreciate
these humorous things. It began to appear more and
more possible to become reconciled to my destiny and
not begrudge myself some of the small joys of life.

Of course, you always feel like that when you've just
returned from Italy. You don't give a hoot about prin-
ciples and prejudices, you smile indulgently, keep your
hands in your pockets, and consider yourself a shrewd
man of the world. For a while you let yourself drift with
the easy, warm life of people in the south and begin to
believe you can go on living like that when you're back
home. Each time I returned from Italy, I felt this way,
and more so on this occasion than on any other. When
I reached Basel, only to find the same old inflexible life
unchanged and unchangeable, I meekly and angrily
descended from my heights step by step. Yet part of
what I had acquired stayed with me. Never after did my

little boat sail through clear or troubled waters without sporting at least one brightly colored, defiantly fluttering, confident pennant.

In other ways, too, many of my views had gradually changed. Without much regret I felt myself outgrowing my adolescence and maturing to the point where life appears a short path, yourself a traveler whose peregrinations and final disappearance are of no great consequence to the world. You keep your eyes fixed on your objective, a favorite dream. But you never consider yourself indispensable and you indulge yourself with rest periods every so often, and don't mind losing an entire day lying down in the grass, whistling a tune and enjoying the present without any thought of the future. Although I had never worshipped Zarathustra, I had been what is known as a *Herrenmensch* and until now had never lacked for self-veneration or been sparing with disdain of my inferiors. Now I began to see that there are no hard and fast boundaries; that life among poor, oppressed, humble people is as varied as life among the distinguished and favored few, and on the whole warmer and more genuine and exemplary.

Besides, I returned to Basel just in time to attend the first soiree at Elizabeth's house—she had been married while I was away. I was in good spirits, still fresh and tanned from my trip, and able to tell any number of amusing anecdotes. The lovely woman seemed to take pleasure in singling me out for her trust. Throughout the evening I rejoiced in my luck at having been spared the disgrace of a belated proposal. For despite my Italian experience, I still harbored the suspicion that women take cruel delight in the hopeless agony of men who are in love with them. I had the liveliest illustration of such a humiliating and painful situation in the form of a story told me by a five-year-old boy. In the school he attended, the following remarkable and symbolic custom was practiced. If one of the boys was guilty of a gross misdemeanor and had to be punished, six girls would be ordered to hold the struggling victim in the required position. Holding the boy was considered a great pleasure and privilege, so the sadistic task was reserved for the six best-behaved girls in class—the moment's paragons of virtue. I have often thought about this amusing childhood anecdote and on occasion it has even crept into my dreams. Thus I know, at least from my dream experience, how miserable a man feels in such a situation.

Chapter Seven

I HAD AS LITTLE RESPECT for my own writing as ever. I was able to live from the proceeds of my work, save small amounts, and even send my father a little money now and then. He cheerfully took it right to the tavern, where he sang my praises. It even occurred to him to do me a favor in return. I once told him that I earned most of my money writing newspaper articles, so he thought I was an editor or reporter of the kind employed by the provincial papers. Now he dictated three letters to me, reporting what he felt were important events that would supply me with copy and income. The first item concerned a barn fire; there followed a report about two tourists who had a mountain-climbing accident; and last, he sent the results of the election for village mayor. These missives were couched in grotesque journalese but made me genuinely happy, for they were a sign of true friendship between us—they were the first letters I had received from home in years. Moreover, I found them refreshing as a kind of unwitting deprecation of my own scribbling, for month after month I reviewed books the importance and consequence of whose publication were minute compared with what happened in the provinces.

Just about that time, books were published by two
writers whom I had known as outrageously lyrical
youths during my days in Zurich. One of them lived in
Berlin now and knew lots of pornographic stories about
café society and the brothels of the capital. The second
had built himself a luxurious hermitage outside Munich, and teetered despicably and hopelessly between
neurotic introspection and spiritist stimulants. I had to
review their books and of course I made harmless fun
of both of them. The neurotic's sole reply was a con-
temptuous letter—written, however, in a truly princely
style. The Berliner made my review the occasion for a
scandal in a literary journal, claiming I had misunderstood his real intent. He invoked Zola's literary princi-
ples and used my unsympathetic review as a basis for
an attack not just on me personally but on the conceited and prosaic nature of the Swiss people as a
whole. As it happens, the man had spent the only
healthy and comparatively dignified period of his literary life in Zurich. I had never been noted for excessive patriotism, but this overdose of Berlin snottiness
was a little too much for me and I sent the malcontent
a letter that did not disguise my contempt for his over-
blown metropolitan modernism.

The quarrel made me feel better and forced me once
more to reevaluate my opinions of modern culture. This
proved tedious and difficult and had few if any pleasant

results. My book will hardly suffer if I omit them. Yet these observations also compelled me to think more deeply about my long-planned life's work.

As you know, it had been my hope to write a work of some length in which I intended to bring closer to people the grandiose and mute life of nature, that they might love it. I wanted to teach people to listen to the pulse of nature, to partake of the wholeness of life and not forget, under the pressure of their petty destinies, that we are not gods and have not created ourselves but are children of the earth, part of the cosmos. I wanted to remind them that night, rivers, oceans, drifting clouds, storms, like creatures of the poet's imagination and of our dreams, are symbols and bearers of our yearning that spread their wings between heaven and earth, their objectives being the indubitable right to life and the immortality of all living things. Each being's innermost core is certain of these rights as a child of God, and reposes without fear in the lap of eternity. Everything evil, sick, and diseased that we carry in us contradicts life and proclaims death. But I also wanted to teach men to find the sources of joy and life in the love of nature. I wanted to preach the pleasures of looking at nature, of wandering in it, and of taking delight in the present.

I wanted to let mountains, oceans, and green islands speak to you convincingly with their enticing tongues, and wanted to compel you to see the immeasurably varied and exuberant life blossoming and overflowing outside your houses and cities each and every day. I wanted you to feel ashamed of knowing more about foreign wars, fashions, gossip, literature, and art than of the springs bursting forth outside your towns, than of the rivers flowing under your bridges, than of the forests and marvelous meadows through which your railroads speed. I wanted to let you know what a golden chain of unforgettable pleasures I, a melancholy recluse, had found in this world and I desired that you, who are perhaps happier and more cheerful than I, should discover even greater joy in it.

Above all, I wanted to implant the secret of love in your hearts. I hoped to teach you to be brothers to all living things, and become so full of love that you will not fear even sorrow and death and receive them like brothers and sisters when they come to you.

All this I hoped to convey not in hymns but truthfully, simply, and factually—with the same combination of seriousness and humor with which a returning traveler tells his friends what he has experienced.

I wanted, I wished, I hoped: I know it sounds odd, but I am still waiting for the day when all this wanting will resolve itself in a form and a plan. I had collected much material, in my head and in the small notebooks I carried with me on my trips and hikes, filling one every few weeks. In these I made brief notations of everything I saw in the world, without reflection or transitions. They are more like painters' sketchbooks and in few words capture concrete, real things: country lanes and well-traveled roads, aspects of mountains and cities, conversations overheard among farmers, artisans, market women, rules by which to forecast the weather, notes on light effects, winds, rain, rocks, plants, animals, the flight of birds, the shapes of waves and clouds, the colors of the sea. Occasionally I constructed short stories around these observations and published them as nature and travel studies, but without relating them to man. The story of a tree, an animal, or the course of a cloud was interesting enough without human scaffolding.

It occurred to me, of course, that a work of such scope without any human figures would be grotesque. Yet for years I strove after this ideal, cherishing the hope that some great inspiration would help me overcome the impossible. I finally realized that I would have to put people in my beautiful landscapes, but I knew I was not able to represent them as they are. I had much ground to make up, and I am making up that lost ground even today. I had always thought of mankind as a mass, as something alien; now I learned the great worth of the individual—not "abstract humanity"—and my notebooks and my memory began to fill up with entirely new sketches.

At first these observations proved rewarding: I shed

my naïve indifference and became interested in a wide range of people. I saw how much of what is everywhere taken for granted was foreign to me; I also realized how greatly my many trips and hikes had opened and sharpened my eyes. And because I have always been drawn to children, it gave me particular pleasure to be in their company.

Still, I found the observation of clouds and waves more enjoyable than the study of mankind. I realized with astonishment that man is distinguished from the rest of nature primarily by a slippery, protective envelope of illusions and lies. In a very short time, I observed this phenomenon among all my acquaintances. It is the result of each person's having to make believe that he is a unique individual, whereas no one really knows his own innermost nature. Somewhat bewildered, I noticed the same trait in myself and I now gave up the attempt to get to the core of people. In most cases the protective envelope was of crucial importance anyway. I found it everywhere, even among children, who, whether consciously or unconsciously, always play a role completely and instinctively instead of displaying who they are.

After a while I began to feel I was making no progress and was wasting my time with trivia. First I sought to locate the fault in myself, yet I could not long deceive myself: I was disillusioned, my environment simply did not provide the people I was searching for. I needed not characters but prototypes, which neither my circle of academicians nor my socialites provided. I thought of Italy with longing, and the friends and companions of my many hikes, the apprentice journey-men. Many a one I walked side by side with had turned out to be a fine fellow.

Visiting the local youth hostel or flophouses was use-less. Drifting hoboes and tramps were of no help to me. So I was at a loss once more, and confined my studies to children. Then I started to hang around taverns, where, of course, I found nothing. There fol-lowed several unhappy weeks in which I doubted my judgment and concluded that my hopes and wishes were exaggerated and ridiculous. I spent much of my time roaming the countryside and brooded away many an evening over wine.

Around that time several stacks of books I would have preferred keeping instead of selling to the second-hand dealer accumulated on my table; there was no room for them on my bookshelves. To solve the prob-lem, I went to see a carpenter and asked him to come to my quarters to take measurements for a bookcase.

One day he came: a slightly built, slow-moving man with a cautious manner. He measured the room, knelt on the floor, extended the measuring stick to the ceil-ing, and painstakingly noted dimension after dimension in inch-high figures in his notebook. He smelled faintly of glue. As he moved about, he jostled an armchair laden with books. A few of them dropped to the floor and he bent down to pick them up. Among them was a pocket dictionary of vocational slang. You can find this paperbound book in almost all lodging houses in Germany frequented by journeying tradesmen. It is a well-edited and delightful little volume.

When the carpenter noticed the familiar book, he shot a curious glance at me, half amused and half suspicious.

"What's the matter?" I asked.

"There's a book here I know. Do you really study it?"

"I studied it while I was out on the road," I replied. "You feel like looking up an expression now and again."

"Really!" he exclaimed. "You've been on the road yourself?"

"Not quite the way you mean. But I've covered a lot of ground on foot and spent many a night in a flophouse."

Meanwhile he had restacked the books and was about to leave. "Where did you get to in your travels?" I asked him.

"From here to Koblenz and later down to Geneva. Wasn't the worst time of my life either."

"Spent a night or two in jail, I suppose?"

"Just once, in Durlach."

"I'd like it if you'd tell me more. We'll meet again, all right, over a glass of wine?"

"I wouldn't care too much for that. But if you'd like you can come up to my place after work and shoot the breeze. I don't mind, provided you're not pulling my leg."

A few days later—Elizabeth was having open house —I stopped in the middle of the street and considered whether I wouldn't rather spend the evening with the carpenter instead. I turned around, went home and left my frock coat, and went to visit him. His workshop was closed and dark inside, and I stumbled through a gloomy hallway and a courtyard and climbed up and down the back staircase several times before finding a sign on a door with the master's name on it. Upon entering, I stepped directly into a tiny kitchen where a gaunt woman was preparing dinner and watching over three children at the same time, so that the narrow room was full of life and considerable noise. Somewhat taken aback, the woman led me into the adjacent room, where the carpenter sat at the window reading his paper in the twilight. First he grumbled, because he mistook me for an overeager client. Then he recognized me and shook my hand.

Because he had been taken by surprise and was embarrassed, I turned to the children, who ran back into the kitchen. I followed them. The sight of the carpenter's wife preparing a rice dish brought back memories of my Umbrian padrona and I lent a hand with the cooking. In our part of the world rice generally is boiled until it turns into a paste lacking all flavor, which sticks to your gums like glue. The same calamity was about to occur here and I saved the meal just in time by reaching for the pot and ladle and taking charge of the preparations myself. The woman submitted to my intrusion in astonishment, the rice turned out passably, she served it, turned on the lamp, and I had a plateful myself.

The carpenter's wife thereupon engaged me in such a detailed conversation about cooking that her husband scarcely got a word in edgewise and had to put off to another evening the story of his adventures as a journeyman apprentice. They sensed soon enough that I was a gentleman in appearance only and basically a farmer's son and the child of ordinary people, and so that first evening we were already on good terms. For just as they recognized me as their equal, I recognized my native atmosphere in this poor household. These people had no time for refinements, for posturing and sentimental charades. Their harsh and demanding life was much too dear for them to adorn it with pretty phrases.

I visited the carpenter more and more often and not only did I forget society's shabby nonsense but also my melancholy and my shortcomings. It was as if I had discovered a piece of my childhood and was continuing the life the monks had interrupted when they sent me to school.

Bent over a torn and yellowing, old-fashioned map, the carpenter and I traced our respective journeys and rejoiced over each city gate and street we both knew. We told all the old traveler's jokes and once even sang some of the old songs. We discussed the difficulties of the trade, the household, the children, the affairs of the city—and gradually our roles were reversed. I was grateful to him and he taught me and gave me something of himself. With immense relief, I felt surrounded by reality, rather than drawing-room noise.

Of his children, his five-year-old daughter caught my eye, because she was especially delicate. Her name was Agnes, and she was called Aggie. She was blond, pale, fragile, and had large, timid eyes and a gentle and shy nature. One Sunday when I came to join the family for a long walk, Aggie was sick. Her mother stayed with her, and we walked slowly to the outskirts of town. Behind St. Margaret's Church we two men sat down on a bench. The children went off in search of flowers, rocks, and bugs, while we surveyed the summer meadows, the Binning cemetery, and the beautiful blue range of the Jura Mountains. The carpenter was tired and depressed.

"What's wrong?" I asked when the children had gone. He looked at me sadly.

"Haven't you seen?" he said. "Aggie's dying. I've known it for a long time, and I'm only surprised she's lived as long as she has. She's always had death in her eyes, and now there's no doubt."

I made an attempt to console him, but soon gave up.

"You see," he smiled sadly, "you don't believe either that she'll live. I'm no fatalist, you know, and I go to church only once in a long while, but I can feel in my bones that the Almighty wants a word with me now. She's only a child, I know, and she's never been well, but God knows I love her more than the others."

Shouting joyously, the children came running up to us with a thousand questions, pressed close to us, asked if I knew the names of weeds and flowers, and finally asked that I tell them a story. So I told them that each of the flowers, trees, and bushes had a soul of its own, like a child and its guardian angel. The father listened too and smiled, and here and there added a word for emphasis. We watched the blue of the mountains grow more intense, heard the tolling of evening bells, and started back. The crimson breath of evening hung over the meadows, the spires of the cathedral pointed small and thin into the warm air, the sky gradually changed from summer blue to a beautiful greenish-golden hue, the trees cast longer and longer shadows. The children were tired and subdued. Perhaps they were thinking of the guardian angels of poppies, pinks, and harebells, while we older ones thought of Aggie, whose soul was about to take wing and leave our timid little band behind.

The next two weeks, all went well. Aggie seemed to be rallying; she was able to leave her bed for a few hours a day and looked prettier and happier, propped on her cool pillows, than ever before. Then there were several feverish nights, and we realized without a word being said that she would not be with us for more than a few days, or a week. Only once did her father speak of it. It was in his workshop. I saw him rummaging about in his stack of boards and knew instinctively that he was selecting pieces for the child's coffin.

"It's a matter of days anyway," he said. "And I'd rather do it after everyone's gone home."

I sat down on one of the benches while he went on working at the other. When the boards were planed smooth, he showed them to me with a kind of pride. He'd used a good, sound, unblemished piece of pine.

"It's not going to be nailed together; I'll make the pieces dovetail, so that it'll be a good, lasting piece of work. But that's enough for today. Let's go on up to the wife."

The midsummer days went by, each warmer and

more lovely than the other, and every day I would sit with Aggie for an hour or two, telling her about lovely meadows and forests, holding her frail hand in my broad palm, my whole being absorbing the sweet clear grace that was hers to the last day.

Then we stood anxiously and sadly by her side, as the small, emaciated body gathered its last strength to wrestle with death; but death vanquished her easily. Her mother remained calm and strong, but her father flung himself across the bed and took a hundred farewells, stroking her blond hair and kissing his dead child.

A brief and simple burial service followed, and then uncomfortable evenings during which we could hear the children weeping in bed in the next room. Then came lovely walks to the cemetery, where we planted flowers on the fresh grave and sat on a bench in the cool grounds, gazing with changed eyes on the earth in which our dear one lay buried, and on the trees that grew above it, and on the birds whose song, uninhibited and as gay as ever, floated through the quiet churchyard.

Simultaneously the strict routine of work took its course, the children began to sing again, fighting among themselves, laughing, and asking for stories, and almost unawares we all became accustomed to not seeing Aggie ever again.

While all this was happening, I did not visit the

professor's house once. I saw Elizabeth only a few times, and on these occasions I felt strangely constrained and at a loss during our tepid conversations. Now I went to visit both houses, only to find them locked for the summer. Everyone had gone to the country long ago. Only then did I realize that my friendship with the carpenter and my preoccupation with the sick child had made me forget all about the hot season and taking a holiday. Before, I would have found it impossible to remain in town in July and August.

I bid Basel goodbye for a short time and set out on a walking tour through the Black Forest. During the trip I had the rare pleasure of sending the carpenter's children picture postcards of all the places I visited, and imagining how I would describe to them everything I was seeing.

In Frankfurt I decided to take a few extra days and went on to Aschaffenburg, Nuremberg, Munich, and Ulm. I took renewed pleasure in the old works of art. Finally I even stopped briefly in Zurich. All these years I had avoided that city as if it were a grave; now I rambled down the familiar streets, sought out the old taverns and beer-gardens, and thought back on the wonderful years I had spent here.

Erminia was married. Someone gave me her address and one evening I went to call on her. I read her husband's name on the door, looked up at the window, and hesitated. Then the old days came alive within me and with a gentle ache my old love was roused out of its slumber. I turned back and did not spoil the idyllic picture of my beloved with a needless reunion. Walking on, I came to the garden by the lake where the artists had held their midsummer fete, and I looked up at the house in whose attic I had spent three years of my life, and from this stream of memories the name Elizabeth suddenly sprang to my lips. My new love was stronger after all than all previous infatuations. It was also quieter, less demanding, more grateful.

Pleased with my mood, I untied one of the boats and rowed with easy, leisurely strokes out onto the warm bright lake. Evening was near and a single lovely snow-white cloud hung high in the sky. I kept my eyes on it, giving it a friendly nod as I thought back on my child-hood love of clouds, on Elizabeth, on that Segantini cloud in front of which I had seen her so beautiful and enraptured. Never before had I felt my love for her—untarnished by a single wrong word or low desire—to be so purifying and ennobling as now. At the sight of this cloud, I gazed back calmly and thankfully on everything good in my life, troubled no longer by the confusions and passions of my adolescence, experienc-ing the old yearning but in a more mature and tranquil way.

I had always sung a tune, or hummed, to the beat of oars on the water. I sang softly to myself now and realized that I was singing verse. I remembered it and

wrote it down at home, as a souvenir of that beautiful
evening on the lake in Zurich:

> *Wie eine weisse Wolke*
> *Am hohen Himmel steht,*
> *So licht und schön und ferne*
> *Bist du, Elisabeth.*

> *Die Wolke geht und wandert,*
> *Kaum hast du ihrer acht,*
> *Und doch durch deine Träume*
> *Geht sie bei dunkler Nacht.*

> *Geht und erglänzt so selig,*
> *Dass fortan ohne Rast*
> *Du nach der weissen Wolke*
> *Ein süsses Heimweh hast.*

["Like the white cloud, high in the sky, you are bright
and beautiful and unattainable, Elizabeth. / The cloud
drifts and wanders off while you look at it, yet in the
dark night it drifts through your dreams / —drifts and
shines so blissfully that forevermore you will ache for
the white cloud with sweet desire."]

On my return to Basel there was a letter for me from
Assisi. It was from Signora Nardini and full of good
news. She had found a second husband after all. But I
think I'll just quote her letter to you:

My very dear Herr Peter!

Allow your faithful friend the liberty of writing to you. It has pleased God to grant me a piece of great good fortune and I would like to invite you to my wedding on the twelfth of October. His name is Menotti. He has little money, yet he loves me very much and knows all about the fruit trade. He is handsome but not as strong and beautiful as you, Herr Peter! He will sell fruit on the piazza while I look after the shop. Lovely Marietta—you remember, our neighbor's girl—is also getting married, but only to a stonemason from out of town.

I think of you every day and have told many people about you. I am very fond of you and have donated four candles to Saint Francis in memory of you. Menotti will be happy too if you come to the wedding. If he gets unfriendly with you then, I'll make him stop. Unfortunately little Matteo Spinelli is really a louse as I always said he was. He always stole lemons from me and now they've taken him away because he stole twelve lire from his father, the baker, and because he poisoned the dog of the beggar Giangiacomo.

I wish you the blessing of God and of Saint Francis. I long to see you.

Your devoted and faithful friend,

Annunziata Nardini

Postscript — Our harvest was so-so. The grapes didn't do well at all, and there weren't enough pears either. But we had plenty of lemons, so many we had to sell them cheap. A horrible accident happened in Spello. A young fellow killed his brother with a rake. No one knows why. He must have been envious of him even though they were brothers.

Unfortunately, I could not accept the invitation, tempting though it was. I sent my best regards and promised to visit in the spring. Then I took a present I had bought for the children in Nuremberg and went to see the carpenter.

There I found a great and unexpected change. Between the window and the table was crouched a grotesque figure in something like a baby's highchair. This was Boppi, the wife's brother, a poor, half-paralyzed hunchback for whom no other place had been found after his mother's death. The carpenter had taken him in quite reluctantly, and the cripple's presence was like a dead-weight on the desolate household. They had not yet grown used to him. The children were frightened; his embarrassed sister pitied him halfheartedly; and her husband was obviously disgruntled.

Boppi had no neck. His was an ugly double hunch on which rested a large, sharp-featured head with a strong nose, a broad forehead, and a beautiful, languishing mouth. His eyes were clear and calm, yet frightened, and his small, delicate hands lay white and unmoving on his narrow breast. I too felt embarrassed and put off by the pathetic intruder. It was uncomfortable to listen to the carpenter recount the invalid's story while he sat in the same room gazing at his hands, neither of us talking to him. He was born crippled but had completed grade school. He had been able to make himself somewhat useful for many years by weaving in straw. Then repeated attacks of gout had partially paralyzed him. For years now, he'd either lain in bed or been propped up on cushions in his strange chair. His sister said she remembered he used to sing beautifully to himself at one time, though sometimes she hadn't heard him sing for years, and never once since he had moved into the house. While all this was being told and discussed, he sat there staring into the distance. I felt ill at ease and soon left and did not come again for some days.

I had been strong and healthy all my life. I had never once been seriously ill and regarded invalids, especially cripples, with pity and with some contempt too. It did not suit me at all to have my leisurely, cheerful life in the bosom of this family disturbed by the coming of this miserable creature. Therefore I postponed my visit from one day to the next and tried vainly to think of a way to get the cripple out of the house. There had to be some inexpensive way of placing him in a hospital or nursing home. A number of times I even thought of going to see the carpenter to talk to him about it. But I hesitated to bring up the subject myself, and I had a childish horror of meeting the invalid. It filled me with revulsion to see him and to shake his hand.

So I let the first Sunday pass and did nothing. The second Sunday, I was all set to take the early-morning train to the Jura Mountains when I felt suddenly ashamed of my cowardice. I stayed home and went to see the carpenter after lunch.

With great reluctance I shook Boppi's hand. The carpenter was in a bad humor and suggested we go for a walk. He said he was fed up with this misery. I was glad to find him in a frame of mind receptive to my suggestion. His wife wanted to stay home, but Boppi asked her to go along with us. He said it was just as well if he was alone. If he had a book to read and a glass of water within reach, they could lock the door behind them and not worry about it.

And we who thought of ourselves as decent, good-hearted people locked him in and went for a walk. And we enjoyed ourselves, had fun with the children, and delighted in the golden autumn sun. We did not feel ashamed or worry about having left the cripple alone in the house. On the contrary, we were glad to be rid of him. With relief we breathed in the clear, sun-warmed air and gave every appearance of being an appreciative,

healthy family enjoying God's Sunday with understanding and gratitude.

Boppi was not mentioned until we were all seated
around a table at an outdoor restaurant. The carpenter
complained what a burden the lodger was, sighed at the
room he took up and the expenses that were incurred
on his account, and finally laughed, saying: "Well, at
least we can be happy for an hour out here without him
disturbing us."

These thoughtless words made me realize that the
helpless cripple, beseeching, suffering Boppi, whom we
did not love, whom we wanted to get rid of, sat sad and
alone, locked in one room. It would be getting dark
shortly and he would be unable to light the lamp or
move closer to the window. He would have to put down
the book and wait in the dark, with no one to talk to or
pass the time with, while we drank wine, laughed, and
enjoyed ourselves. And then I remembered that I had
told the neighbors in Assisi about St. Francis and had
boasted that he had taught me to love all mankind.
Why had I studied the saint's life and learned by heart
his hymn to love and tried to retrace his footsteps in the
Umbrian hills, when I allowed a poor and helpless
creature to lay there suffering though I could help him?

The weight of an invisible, mighty hand fell on my
heart, crushing it with shame and hurt, and I began
to tremble. I knew that God wanted a word with me.

"You love a household," he said, "where people treat you well and where you spend many happy hours. And the day I grace this house with my presence, you run off and scheme to drive me out! You saint, you prophet, you poet!"

I felt as though I were gazing at myself in a clear and infallible mirror where I could see that I was a liar, a braggart, a coward and perjurer. It hurt, it was bitter, humiliating, and horrible. But what hurt in me and suffered agonies and reared up in pain deserved to be broken and destroyed.

Abruptly I rose and left, finishing neither my wine nor my bread, and rushed back to town. In my excitement I was tortured by the unbearable fear that something might have happened to Boppi: there might have been a fire; he might have fallen from his chair, might lie suffering, perhaps dying, on the floor. I could see him lying there, myself standing by his side, forced to endure the cripple's reproachful looks.

Breathlessly I reached the house and stormed up the stairs. Then it occurred to me that the door was locked and I had no key. Yet my fear subsided at once, for even before I reached the door I heard singing inside. It was a strange moment. With trembling heart and completely out of breath I stood on the dark landing and listened to the cripple's singing within. Slowly I calmed down. He sang softly and gently and somewhat mournfully. It was a popular love song, "Flowers, pink and white." I knew that he had not sung for a long time and I was deeply moved that he used this quiet hour alone to be happy for a while in his own way.

That's the way it is: life loves to put serious and deeply emotional events in a humorous context. I perceived at once how shameful and ridiculous my position was. In my panic I had run for miles, only to find myself without a key. Now I could either leave again or shout my good intentions through two closed doors. I stood on the stairs, wanting to console the poor fellow, to show him my sympathy and help him pass the time, while he sat inside, unaware of my presence, singing. It undoubtedly would only have frightened him if I had called attention to myself by knocking or shouting.

So I had no choice but to leave. I strolled for an hour through the streets and the Sunday crowds, then I found that the family had returned. This time I shook Boppi's hand without reluctance. I sat down next to him, engaged him in conversation, and asked what he was reading. It seemed natural to offer him some books to read, and he thanked me for that. When I suggested Jeremias Gotthelf, it turned out that he was familiar with his work. Gottfried Keller, however, was unknown to him and I promised to lend him some of Keller's books.

Next day when I brought the books I had a chance to

be alone with him, for his sister was just going out and her husband was in the workshop. I confessed how ashamed I felt for leaving him alone the day before and said I would be glad to sit with him sometimes and be his friend.

The invalid turned his large head slightly in my direction, looked at me, and said, "Thank you." That was all. But for him to turn his head was a great effort; it was as if I had received tenfold embraces from someone healthy. And his eyes were so bright and innocent that I blushed with shame.

Now I faced the more difficult task of speaking to the carpenter. The best course seemed to be an outright confession of my fear and shame of yesterday. Unfortunately, he did not understand what I had in mind, but at least he was willing to discuss it. Finally he accepted my proposal that the cripple should be our mutual responsibility, that we would share the trifling expense of keeping him, and I received permission to visit him whenever I wished. I was free to consider him my brother.

Fall was warm and beautiful for an exceptionally long time that year. That was why the first thing I did was buy Boppi a wheelchair and take him out every day, mostly in the company of the children.

Chapter Eight

IT SEEMS to have been my bad luck always to receive more than I could return, from life and friends. It had been that way with Richard, Elizabeth, Signora Nardini, and it had been so with the carpenter. Now, a full-grown man who did not think all that badly of himself, I found myself the astonished and grateful pupil of a wretched cripple. If ever the time comes when I complete and publish the work I started so long ago, it will contain little of value not learned from Boppi. This was the beginning of a good and happy period in my life, and I have drawn sustenance from it ever since. I was granted the privilege of gazing clearly and deeply into a magnificent soul left unscathed by illness, loneliness, poverty, and maltreatment.

All the petty vices that spoil and embitter our beautiful, brief lives—anger, impatience, mistrust, lies, all these insufferable, festering sores that disfigure us—had been burned out of this man through long, intense suffering. He was no sage or angel but a person full of understanding and generosity who, under the stress of horrible agonies and deprivations, had learned to accept being weak and to commit himself into God's hands without being ashamed.

I once asked him how he came to terms with his weak and pain-racked body.

"It's quite simple," he replied, laughing. "I wage a perpetual war with my illness. Sometimes I win an encounter, sometimes I lose one, and we go on skirmishing anyway. At times we both withdraw and there is a temporary cease-fire, but we each lie in wait for the other to become impudent, then we start in all over again."

I had always felt that I had an unerring eye, that I was a good observer. But Boppi taught me even there. He loved nature, especially animals, and so I frequently took him to the zoo. There we spent delightful hours. Before long, Boppi knew them all and, as we always took bread and sugar, some animals came to recognize us, and we made all kinds of friends. Oddly enough, we were particularly fond of the tapir. His only virtue, which he did not share with the rest of the animals, was a certain cleanliness. Otherwise we found him unintelligent, unfriendly, ungrateful, and an extreme glutton. Other animals, the elephant, deer, and chamois in particular, even the ragged bison, always showed some sign of gratitude for the sugar they received: either they threw us a grateful look or they allowed me to pet them. The tapir gave no such indication at all. As soon as we approached, he promptly appeared at his fence, chewed slowly and methodically what we gave him and, when he saw that we had no more, went off without as much as blinking an eye. Since he neither begged nor thanked us for what we gave him but accepted it routinely, like a natural tribute, we took this to be a sign of pride and character and called him the customs collector.

Since Boppi was usually in no position to feed the animals himself, we sometimes fell to debating whether the tapir had had his due, or whether we should let him levy another tidbit. We gave this the most dispassionate consideration, as though it involved a matter of state policy. Once, after we left the tapir, Boppi felt we should have given him one more lump of sugar, so we turned back. But the tapir, comfortable again on his straw, merely squinted haughtily and refused to come to the fence. "Excuse me, Mr. Customs Collector," Boppi called to him, "but I believe we short-changed you one lump." So we went on to the elephant. Waddling back and forth expectanly, he extended his warm, pliant trunk in welcome. Boppi was able to feed the elephant himself and he watched with childish glee as the giant swung out his limber trunk, picking the bread out of Boppi's flat, outstretched hand, squinting slyly and benignly at us out of tiny, merry eyes.

I reached an agreement with one of the keepers that

Boppi could sit at the zoo in his wheelchair when I had no time to stay with him, so he'd be able to get the sun and watch the animals. When I came to fetch him, he would describe everything he had seen during the day. What particularly impressed him was how courteously the lion treated the lioness. As soon as she lay down to rest, the lion redirected his restless pacing so as not to brush against her or have to step over her. Most entertaining for him were the acrobatics of the otter. He never tired of the agile water sports this lithe creature indulged in, as Boppi sat motionless in the chair, each movement of his head or arms costing him great effort.

On one of the most beautiful days that fall, I told Boppi the story of my two loves. We were on such intimate terms now that I felt I could no longer keep from him even the less pleasing and salutary events of my life. He listened gravely and sympathetically but made no comment. Later he confessed a desire to see Elizabeth and asked me not to forget, should we ever come across her on the street.

As this did not happen and the days were turning chilly, I called on Elizabeth and asked her to give the hunchback the pleasure of seeing her. She kindly consented to my request and one day she had me fetch her and take her to the zoo, where Boppi waited for us in his wheelchair. As the lovely, elegantly dressed lady shook the cripple's hand, bending down to him a little, and poor Boppi looked up at her gratefully and almost tenderly with his big kind eyes, I could not decide which of them was more beautiful at this moment or dearer to my heart. Elizabeth said a few kind words to him, and the cripple never once took his shining eyes off her. I stood by, astonished to see the two persons I loved most, and whose lives were divided by such a deep gulf, standing hand in hand before me. Boppi did not speak of anything else except Elizabeth the entire afternoon, praised her beauty, her distinction, her goodness, her walk, her dress, her yellow gloves, her green shoes, her voice, and her pretty hat. But it struck me as painful and grotesque to stand by and watch as the woman I loved handed out alms of kindness to my best friend.

Meantime, Boppi had read Keller's *Der Grüne Heinrich* and *Die Leute von Seldwyla*. He felt so much at home in the world of these unique books that Schmoller Pankraz, Albertus Zwiehan, and the self-righteous combmakers had become our mutual friends. For a while I considered giving Boppi some of Conrad Ferdinand Meyer's books, but it seemed unlikely that he would care for the almost Latin terseness of the style. I also had my doubts about opening the abyss of history before his cheerful, calm eyes. Instead, I told him about St. Francis and gave him Mörike's stories to read.

It was amusing to see how we gradually began addressing each other in the second person singular.

(173

Actually, I had never asked or offered to use the "thou" with him, nor would he have accepted. It all happened quite naturally; we realized we were using it one day and we couldn't help smiling, so we let it continue.

When winter put a stop to our excursions and I again spent entire evenings in the carpenter's living room, I noticed belatedly that my new friendship had been won at some cost, for the carpenter was now grumpy, unfriendly, or simply taciturn. The irksome presence of the useless lodger he had to feed irritated him as much as my friendship with Boppi. Sometimes I would sit an entire evening, chatting gaily with the cripple, while the master of the house grouchily read his paper. Even his wife, usually a model of patience, became cross with her husband; this time she insisted on having her way and not sending Boppi elsewhere. I made several attempts to mollify the carpenter and to suggest alternative solutions, but he seemed permanently disgruntled. He grew caustic and began to jeer at my friendship with the cripple and make life miserable for him. The invalid and I, sitting with him much of the time, were both a burden to the household, which was too crowded even without us. Still, I had not given up hope that the carpenter would some day become as fond of Boppi as I. Finally, however, it became impossible for me to take a step without either offending the carpenter or making Boppi unhappy. Since I have always had an abhorrence of making swift or binding decisions—Richard used to call me Petrus Cunctator, even in Zurich—I waited for weeks, afraid that I might lose the friendship of either, and perhaps of both.

The increasing discomfort of this disruptive situation drove me to my old haunts, the taverns. One evening, after the whole loathsome business had made me particularly angry, I sought refuge in a small Vaudois wine-hall where I exorcised my misery with several liters of wine. For the first time in two years I had some difficulty navigating home in an upright position. As usual after a hard bout of drinking, my mood the next day was cool and easy and I plucked up courage and went to see the carpenter to put an end to this farce once and for all. I suggested he leave Boppi entirely in my hands. He seemed agreeable and finally, after mulling it over a few days, he gave his consent.

Soon after, I moved with my crippled friend into a newly rented apartment. I felt almost as if I were married, since I now had to take care of a real household, not just a makeshift bachelor's quarters. But it all worked out well, though some of my first housekeeping experiments misfired. We had a girl come in every day to clean up and do the laundry. Food was delivered to the house, and soon both of us felt quite comfortable in our new quarters. The prospect of having to give up my hikes and carefree excursions did not worry me yet. I

(175

even found that my friend's presence had a calming, productive effect on my work. All the little services Boppi required were, of course, new to me and I did not find them pleasant at first, particularly the dressing and undressing. But he was so patient and grateful that he made me feel ashamed and I took great care in looking after him.

Recently I had called only rarely at the professor's house, more frequently at Elizabeth's, which, despite everything that had happened, held a continuing fascination for me. There I would drink tea or a glass of wine, watch Elizabeth play hostess, and be overcome occasionally by bouts of sentimentality, though I was always ready to pounce with derision on any Werther-like feelings in myself. Insipid, adolescent selfishness in love, however, had disappeared for good. A delicate and intimate state of war was just the right relationship between Elizabeth and me and we seldom met without engaging in the friendliest of quarrels. The lively and, in a feminine way, illogical turn of mind of that clever woman and my own amorous yet rough-hewn nature were not ill-matched, and since we felt a genuine respect for each other, we would allow ourselves to be at loggerheads, that much more fiercely, over trifles. What struck me as particularly amusing was my defense of the state of bachelorhood to her, the woman to whom I would have offered my life in marriage only a short while before. I was even able to tease her about her husband, who was a thoroughly decent fellow and proud of his clever wife.

Underneath, my old love for her burned. However, the old flame was now replaced by the glow of lasting embers that keep the heart young and before which a confirmed bachelor can warm his hands occasionally on winter nights. Since Boppi had become my friend and I was aware of his constant and honest affection for me, I could safely let my old love linger as a part of my youth and poetry. Besides, every so often Elizabeth's cattiness cooled me off and made me feel grateful for my bachelorhood.

After Boppi and I began to live together, I neglected Elizabeth's house more and more. I read books with Boppi, leafed through travel albums and diaries, and played dominoes. To liven things up a bit, we even bought a poodle. We watched the first signs of winter through our window and each day engaged in clever conversations and silly ones. The invalid had acquired an exalted view of the world, a pragmatic attitude enriched by kindness and humor, from which I learned something every day. When it snowed and winter unfolded its pure loveliness outside the window, we would sit inside by the stove and fashion a safe cocoon for ourselves. The fine art of observing mankind, which hitherto had cost me so many miles on foot, I now pursued effortlessly at Boppi's side. For Boppi, a quiet and acute observer, was filled with pictures of his previous surroundings and, once he got started, could tell marvelous stories. During his entire existence he had probably known no more than three dozen people and had never been part of the mainstream of life, yet he knew life much more accurately than I, for he was accustomed to noticing even the smallest details and finding in every person a source of experience, joy, and understanding.

The pleasure we derived from animals continued to provide our favorite amusement. Now that we could not visit the zoo, we invented stories and fables about them. We did not tell each other the stories; they developed spontaneously in the form of dialogues. For example, a declaration of love between two parrots, a family of bisons quarreling, or evening conversations among the boars.

"How're things, Mr. Marten?"

"So-so, Mr. Fox. You will remember the time I was captured and lost my beloved wife, Bush Tail was her name as I've had the pleasure of informing you previously. A pearl of a girl, I can assure you . . ."

"Oh, neighbor, forget all those old stories. You must have talked about this pearl business a hundred times.

CHAPTER EIGHT

My God, we've only one life and we don't want to spoil
the few pleasures we have left by being sentimental."

"As you like, Mr. Fox. But if you'd known my wife,
you wouldn't dare talk like that."

"Of course, of course. So she was called Bush Tail,
right? A fine name, something you can caress! But
what I really wanted to say is this: have you noticed
how the sparrows are plaguing us again? I've got a little
plan."

"For the sparrows?"

"Yes, it's designed for the sparrows. Look—this, I
think, will be our best strategy. We'll put some bread in
front of the bars, lie down, and wait quietly for the little
beggars. I'll be surprised if we don't catch one of them
that way. What do you think?"

"An excellent idea, neighbor."

"Would you be so good as to put a little bread right
over there? Yes, that's fine. But perhaps you ought to
push it a little to the right, then we'll both have a
chance when they come. Pay attention now. We'll lie
down flat, close our eyes . . . but, hush, there's one
homing in on us now." (*Pause.*)

"Well, Mr. Fox, nothing so far?"

"How impatient you are! As if this were the first time
you've hunted! A hunter's main asset is the ability to
wait and wait and wait again. Once more now!"

"Well, where's that bread gone to?"

"Pardon me?"

"The bread, it's gone!"

"Well, I'll be . . . Now, really! The bread? Indeed, it's gone! Well, I'll be damned. It must be the wind again."

"Well, I have an idea I heard you chewing something a while back."

"What? Me chewing?"

"The bread, obviously!"

"Your accusations are becoming insulting, Marten. One has to accept a harsh remark or two from a neighbor, but that's going too far! I repeat, too far! Do you understand? So I'm supposed to have eaten the bread? What's the big idea? First I have to listen to that insipid story about your pearly Bush Tail for the thousandth time, then I have the brilliant notion of putting the bait out there . . ."

"But that was mine! That was my bread!"

". . . putting the bait out there. I lie down and watch. Everything is going fine, then you start your chatter, the sparrows fly off, the hunt is ruined, and now I'm even accused of eating the bread. Well, I declare! You can wait until hell freezes over before I speak another word to you."

Thus our afternoons and evenings passed swiftly and easily. I was in the best of spirits, enjoyed my work, and was surprised that I had been so lazy, discontented, and sluggish before. Even the best times with Richard were no match for these quiet, cheerful days when the snowflakes danced outside the window and we and our poodle huddled around the stove.

And then my beloved Boppi had to commit his first, and last, act of stupidity. In my content, I was inattentive and did not notice that Boppi was experiencing more pain than usual. He, however, out of sheer modesty and affection, assumed a more cheerful air than ever, never uttered a single complaint, did not even ask me not to smoke, and then lay in bed at night suffering, coughing, and groaning softly. Quite by chance, as I was writing late one night in the next room, when he thought I had gone to sleep, I heard him groan. The poor fellow was thunderstruck when I entered the room, lamp in hand. I put the lamp down and sat next to him on the bed and conducted an inquisition. For a time he tried to evade the issue.

"It isn't all that bad," he said finally, with some hesitation. "Only a tightness around the heart when I move in a certain way, and sometimes also when I breathe."

He was literally apologizing, as though his illness were a crime.

Next morning I went to see a doctor. It was a clear, ice-cold day and my anxiety lessened as I walked. I even thought of Christmas and what I might get Boppi. I found the doctor at home and he came at once. We drove to my place in his comfortable carriage, walked up the stairs, entered Boppi's room, and the doctor began his soundings and auscultations. As his voice became more serious and kinder, all my optimism left me.

Gout, a weak heart, a serious case. I listened and wrote everything down and was surprised to find myself making no objection when the doctor ordered Boppi's transfer to the hospital.

The ambulance came in the afternoon. When I returned from the hospital, I felt ghastly in the apartment, with the poodle pressing against me, the invalid's big chair set to one side, and the next room empty.

That's the way it is when you love. It makes you suffer, and I have suffered much in the years since. But it matters little that you suffer, so long as you feel alive with a sense of the close bond that connects all living things, so long as love does not die! I would gladly exchange every happy day of my life, all my infatuations and great plans, provided I could exchange them for gazing deeply once more into this most sacred experience. It bitterly hurts your eyes and heart, and your pride and self-esteem don't get off scot-free either, but afterwards you feel so calm and serene, so much wiser and alive.

Little fair-haired Aggie had taken one part of my old self with her into the grave. Now I saw my dear hunchback, whom I had given all my love and with whom I had shared my whole life, suffer and die bit by bit. I suffered with him and partook of all the terror and sanctity of death. I was still an apprentice in the *ars amandi* and now I had one of my first sad lessons in the *ars moriendi*. I will not be silent about this period of my life, as I was about my days in Paris. I want to speak loud and clear about it—like a woman about her honeymoon or an old man about his boyhood.

I watched a man die whose entire life had consisted of love and pain. I listened to him make jokes like a child, while death was at work in him. I saw his pained eyes seek out mine, not to beg for pity but to strengthen me and to show me that his pain and agonies had not touched the best in him. At those moments his eyes grew wide. You no longer saw his withered face, only the glow in his eyes.

"Is there anything I can do for you, Boppi?"

"Tell me something. Talk about the tapir."

So I talked about the tapir. He closed his eyes and I found it difficult to speak normally, because I was so close to tears. And when I thought he was no longer listening or had fallen asleep, I would stop. Then he would open his eyes again.

"And what happened then . . . ?"

And I went on telling him about the tapir, the poodle,

my father, about wicked little Matteo Spinelli, or about Elizabeth.

"Yes, she married the wrong man. That's the way it goes, Peter."

Often, he would suddenly start talking about dying.

"It's no fun, Peter. Nothing in the world is as difficult as dying. But still you manage it."

Or: "I'll actually have reason to laugh, once this torture is over. Dying is really worth it in my case. I'll be getting rid of a hunched back, a clubfoot, and a stiff hip. It'll be a pity when *you* die—with your broad shoulders and fine, strong legs."

And once, in his last days, he woke from a brief sleep and said, quite loudly: "The priests' heaven doesn't exist. Heaven is far more beautiful than that. Far more."

The carpenter's wife visited him often and was kind and helpful in a sensible way. To my deep regret, the carpenter himself did not come even once.

"What do you think, Boppi?" I would ask him. "Will there be a tapir in heaven, too?"

"Oh, definitely," he said, and nodded. "There's every kind of animal there, even the chamois!"

Christmas came and we had a little celebration at his bedside. A cold wave set in, then a thaw, then fresh snow covered the slippery streets, but I did not really see any of it. I heard, and immediately forgot, that

Elizabeth had given birth to a son. An amusing letter from Signora Nardini arrived; I read it quickly and put it aside. I finished my work in brief, frantic bursts, always aware that each hour I worked was that much less time spent with Boppi. Then I rushed to the hospital, where I would find an atmosphere of serene calm. And I would sit for half a day by Boppi's bed, enveloped in a deep, dreamlike peace.

Shortly before he died, he had a few days when he felt better. It was remarkable how the immediate past seemed to have been blotted out in his memory: he lived entirely in his early years. For two days he spoke only of his mother. He could not talk for long at a time, but it was obvious even in the hour-long pauses that he was thinking of her.

"I've told you far too little about her," he said sadly. "You mustn't forget what I tell you about her; otherwise there'll soon be no one left to remember her and be grateful to her. You see, Peter, it would be a wonderful thing if everyone had a mother like that. She did not have me put in an institution when I couldn't work any longer."

He lay there, breathing with difficulty. An hour passed, then he continued.

"She loved me best of all her children and kept me with her until she died. My brothers emigrated and my sister married the carpenter, but I stayed at home. As poor as my mother was, she never held it against me. You mustn't forget my mother, Peter. She was very tiny, even smaller than I perhaps. When she put her hand in mine, it was just as if a tiny bird had perched on it. 'A child's coffin will be large enough for her,' that's what neighbor Rütiman said when she died."

He would fit in a child's coffin too. He lay small and shrunken in his clean hospital bed, and his hands now looked like those of a languishing woman, long, slender, white, and a little gnarled. When he stopped daydreaming of his mother, he became preoccupied with me. He talked about me as if I were not there beside him.

"He's not had much luck, of course, but it didn't really do him any harm. His mother died too early."

"Don't you recognize me any longer, Boppi?"

"Yes, Herr Camenzind," he said jokingly, and laughed very softly.

The last day, he asked: "Listen, is it very expensive to be in the hospital? It could get to be too expensive."

But he did not expect a reply. A delicate blush spread over his wan face, he closed his eyes and for a while looked supremely happy.

"He is approaching the end," said the nurse.

But he opened his eyes once more, gave me a roguish look, and moved his eyebrows as if trying to reassure me. I stood up, placed my hand under his left shoulder, and lifted him a little, which always afforded him some relief. Leaning against my hand, he let his lips twist once more briefly in pain, then he turned his head a little and shuddered, as though suddenly cold. That was his deliverance.

"Is it all right this way?" I asked him still. But he was free of all suffering. It was one o'clock in the afternoon of the seventh of January. Toward evening we made everything ready. The tiny misshapen body lay peaceful and clean, without further distortion, until it came time for him to be taken away to be buried. During the next two days I was amazed to find myself neither particularly sad nor distressed. I did not weep once. I had experienced parting and separation so deeply during his illness that I had little feeling left now. My grief subsided slowly as I regained my balance.

Still, it seemed a good moment to leave town quietly and find a place somewhere, if possible in the south, to rest and take up the loosely woven threads of my long poem and tighten them on the loom. I still had a little money, so I was able to put off my various literary commitments. I prepared to pack and leave with the first signs of spring. First I would go to Assisi, where Signora Nardini was expecting me. Then I intended to retreat to a quiet mountain hamlet for a stint of good, hard work. It seemed to me that I'd seen enough of life and death now to allow me to presume that people would listen to me if I decided to hold forth on these subjects. Impatiently I waited for March and in anticipation my ears hummed with earthy Italian expressions, and my nose tingled with the aroma of risotto, oranges and Chianti. My plan seemed flawless; the more I thought about it, the better I liked it. However, I did well to savor the Chianti in my imagination, for everything turned out differently.

In February a troubled, fantastically phrased letter from innkeeper Nydegger announced that there had been a heavy snowfall and that something was wrong in the village, with animals as well as people. My father's condition being particularly doubtful, all in all it would be a good thing if I could send some money, or best of all could come myself. Because sending money was not convenient for me and because I was worried about the old man, I had no choice but to go home. I arrived on a thoroughly unpleasant day. On account of the snow and wind, I could make out neither mountains nor houses. I was lucky that I knew my way about so well I could have found my house blindfolded.

Old Camenzind was not bedridden, as I had expected. He sat miserable and meek by the stove, besieged by a neighbor woman who had brought him milk and took the opportunity to lecture him thoroughly and at length on his evil ways, something my arrival did not interrupt.

"Look, Peter's back," announced the hoary sinner, winking at me with his left eye.

But she went right on with her sermon. I sat down on a chair, waiting for her attack of excessive neighborliness to subside, though she made several points in her harangue which it would have done me no harm to pursue. But I just sat there, watching the snow melt on my coat and boots, and form a moist patch, then a little pool, around my chair. Not until the woman was done did we celebrate our reunion officially. The woman joined in amiably and with surprising good grace.

My father had grown much weaker. I thought back on my previous attempt to care for him. Apparently it was no help to leave him alone as I had done; the problem of caring for him had now become more serious and urgent than ever.

After all, you can't expect a gnarled old farmer who was no model of virtue even during his best days to become meek in his dotage or be deeply moved by the sudden spectacle of filial love. And that, of course, was about the last thing my father was going to let happen. Yet the feebler he became, the more loathsome he was. He paid me back for all I ever made him suffer, if not with interest at least in full and equal measure. He was sparing and cautious with remarks addressed to me, but he had access to numerous more drastic measures when disgruntled or bitter—he did not need to say a single word. There were moments when I wondered whether I, too, would turn into such a grouchy crank in my old age. My father's drinking days, however, were virtually over. The glass of good southern wine I poured for him twice a day he enjoyed with ill grace, because I always took the bottle right back down to the cellar and never entrusted him with the key.

Not until the end of February did we have those luminous weeks that make winter in the high Alps such a marvelous spectacle. The high, snow-covered mountains stood out clearly against the cornflower-blue sky and seemed improbably close in the clear air. Meadows and slopes lay covered with that winter mountain snow which is white, grainy, and dry as no snow ever is in the lowland valleys. The sun glistened at noon on swells in the ground. In the hollows and along the slopes lay rich blue shadows. After weeks of snowstorms the air was so clean that each breath was exhilarating. Children were sledding down some of the less formidable slopes, and between noon and one o'clock you could see the old people standing in the street treating themselves to some sun. At night the rafters creaked with the frost. Amid the snowfields lay the tranquil blue lake that never freezes, looking lovelier than it ever did in summer.

Each day before lunch I would help my father out of the house and watch him stretch his brown, gnarled hands in the sun. After a while he would begin to cough and complain that he felt chilly. This was one of his harmless tricks for getting me to fetch him a glass of schnapps, for neither cough nor chill could be taken seriously. Thus he received a small glass of gentian schnapps or absinthe. In artfully graduated steps he ceased coughing as he secretly congratulated himself on having outwitted me once again. After lunch I would leave him, strap on my leggings, and climb up into the mountains for a few hours, going as high as the time allowed, then return by way of a fruit sack I'd taken along, sitting on it and tobogganing home across sloping fields of snow.

By the time I had intended to set out for Assisi, the snow was still several feet deep. In April, spring finally began to make itself felt, bringing with it a thaw as swift and dangerous as any our village had experienced for years. Day and night you could hear the Föhn howl, distant avalanches crash, and the embittered roar of torrents carrying boulders and splintered trees, hurling them on our narrow strips of land and orchards. The Föhn fever would not let me sleep. Night after night, rapt and fearful I heard the storm moan, the avalanches thunder, the raging water of the lake burst against the shore.

During this period of feverish springtime battles, I was once more overcome by my old love sickness, so impetuously this time that I got up at night, leaned out the window, and bellowed words of love out into the storm to Elizabeth. Since that warm night when I had gone mad with love on the hill above Erminia's house, passion had not possessed me as horribly and irresistibly as this. It seemed to me often as if the beautiful woman were standing very close, smiling at me, yet withdrawing with each step I took in her direction. All my thoughts invariably returned to this image. Like an infected man, I could not help scratching the itching sore. I was ashamed of myself, but this was as agonizing as it was futile. I damned the Föhn, but all my agonies were accompanied secretly by the half-hidden warmth of lust, as I had felt it during my boyhood longing for Rösi Girtanner. The dark warm wave of passion flooded over me.

I realized that this malady was incurable and tried to do a little work at least. I drew up a master plan and drafted several preliminary studies, but soon I saw that this was not the right time. Meanwhile, ominous reports of the Föhn were coming in from all quarters and the village itself was badly stricken. Dams along the raging brooks broke; houses, barns, and stables were heavily damaged; and several families in outlying districts, deprived of any shelter, sought refuge with us. Everywhere there was lamentation and distress and nowhere was there any money. It was my good fortune that the mayor asked me to his office to see if I would be willing to join the relief committee. He felt confident that I would be able to represent the village successfully before the cantonal government and arouse the rest of the country with newspaper articles asking for help and money. The request came just at the right moment, for it suited me to be able to forget my own unproductive suffering by engaging in more serious and worthwhile affairs. So I threw myself into the cause with all my heart. By means of a few letters, I quickly found several people in Basel willing to collect money for us. The cantonal government, as we knew, had no funds and only sent a few people to help us. Then I turned to the newspapers, with reports and demands: letters, contributions, and inquiries poured in. In addition to attending to this massive correspondence, I had to contend with the hard-nosed farmers who served on the community council.

These few weeks of disciplined, strenuous work were very good for me. By the time the operation was running fairly smoothly and my services were less necessary, the meadows were turning green all around us, and the lake again reflected sun and snow-free slopes.

My father was a little improved and my love sickness had disappeared like the soiled remains of an avalanche. This was the time of year when my father used to repair his boat, while Mother watched from the garden, and I too watched, my eyes trained on his agile hands, on the smoke curling from his pipe, and on the yellow butterflies. Now there was no boat in need of a paint job, Mother had died long ago, and my father huddled moodily in our derelict house.

Uncle Konrad also reminded me of the old days. Sometimes, without Father seeing us, I would take him to the inn for a glass of wine and listen to him reminisce with good-humored laughter, and not without pride, about his many ventures. He no longer engaged in adventures, and old age had left its mark on him in other ways too, though his face and laugh still had a certain boyishness that always pleased me. Often, when I became fed up with my father, he was my sole consolation and amusement. When I took him to the inn for a glass of wine, he trotted by my side and tried his best to keep his thin, crooked legs in step with mine.

"Hoist your sails, Uncle Konrad," I would say encouragingly, and at the word "sail" we invariably began to discuss our old boat, now gone, mourning it like a lost friend. As I had been fond of the old wreck and missed it, we dredged up all the stories about it in great detail.

The lake was as blue as ever, the sun no less festive and warm. Older by so many years, I often contemplated the yellow butterflies with a feeling that had changed very little. Couldn't I lie down in the meadows again and abandon myself to dreams? That this was no

longer possible became obvious to me whenever I
washed: I saw my face with its prominent nose and
sour mouth smiling back at me out of the rusty wash-
basin. Camenzind Senior made even more certain that I
would make no mistake about the way times had
changed. If I wanted to be transported into the present,
all I needed to do was open the tightly-wedged table
drawer in my room, where my future work lay slumbering, a package of outdated sketches and six or seven
drafts on quarto sheets. But I opened this drawer only
rarely.

Besides caring for the old man, I had my hands full
with our decrepit house. There were gaping holes in the
floorboards, oven and stove were defective, smoke filled
the rooms with acrid stench, the doors would not shut
properly, and the ladder to the loft, once the scene of
my father's chastisements, was a danger to life and
limb. Before I could undertake any repairs, I had to
have the ax ground, the saw sharpened, borrow a
hammer, and find some nails. The next problem was to
fashion usable pieces of wood from the remains of our
rotting stock. Uncle Konrad lent a hand with repairing
the tools and the old grindstone, yet he was too old and
bent to be of much use. So I tore my tissue-soft writer's
hands on the splintery wood, worked the wobbly grindstone treadle, clambered over the leaky roof, nailed,
hammered, cut the tiles, and whittled away. During all

this I lost a considerable portion of my excess weight. At times, especially while wearily patching the roof, I would suddenly come to a halt, the hammer in midair, and sit down to take a pull on my half-extinguished cigar and gaze into the deep blue sky. I savored my idleness, glad that my father could no longer goad me or find fault. If neighbors happened to pass by, women, old men, or schoolchildren, I would amplify my inactivity by engaging them in neighborly chats. Gradually I earned the reputation of being someone you could talk to sensibly.

"It's warm, Lizbeth, isn't it?"

"Right you are, Peter. What's that you're doing?"

"Patching the old roof."

"Can't do it any harm. It's been needing it for so long now."

"Right you are, Lizbeth."

"What's the old man up to these days? He must be seventy if he's a day."

"Eighty, Lizbeth, eighty it is. What do you think it'll be like when we're as old as that? It's no fun."

"Right you are, Peter. But I've got to get on now. My man wants his lunch. Take care now."

"Bye now, Lizbeth."

And as she walked on with her lunch basket, I blew smoke clouds in the air, followed her with my eyes, and wondered how it was that everyone else accomplished so much while I had been hammering away at the same plank for two full days. But finally the roof was patched. For once, my father took an interest, and as I couldn't hoist him up to the roof, I had to produce a detailed account of every board I had replaced. It didn't really matter that I exaggerated a little.

"That's fine," my father conceded. "That's fine, but I never would have believed you'd get it done this year."

When I reflect on all my journeys and efforts to live, I am both pleased and annoyed to have proved the old adage that "fish belong in the water, farmers on the land." No amount of art will transform a Camenzind from Nimikon into a city dweller. It is a situation to which I am becoming accustomed, and I am glad that my clumsy pursuit of luck has led me back, against my will, to the old nook between lake and mountains where I started, and where the virtues and vices, especially the latter, are the normal, traditional ones. In the world outside I had forgotten what it was like at home and had come very near to regarding myself as some rare and remarkable bird. Now I saw once again that it was merely the spirit of Nimikon spooking about inside me, unable to adjust to the customs of the rest of the world. Here in my village, no one thinks of me as out-of-the-ordinary. When I look at my father, or at Uncle Konrad, I feel myself to be a very normal son and nephew.

My few flings in the realm of intellect, and the so-called world of culture, can be compared to my uncle's famous sailing episode—except that they cost me more in money, effort, and precious years. My appearance too, now that Cousin Kuoni trims my beard and I walk around again in lederhosen and rolled-up sleeves, has become completely native. When I am old and gray, I will take my father's place and play his small role in village life and no one will notice. People know only that I was away for many years. I take great care not to tell them what a miserable life I led then, and how often I got stuck—otherwise they'd have a nickname for me in no time at all. Whenever I tell any of them about Germany, Italy, or Paris, I boast a little. Sometimes I begin to doubt my own veracity even in the well-remembered parts of my stories.

What, then, is the upshot of so many blind voyages and wasted years? The woman I loved and still love is rearing her two beautiful children in Basel. The other woman, who loved me, has found consolation and carries on her fruit, vegetable, and seed trade. My father, for whose sake I returned to this God-forsaken haven, has neither deteriorated completely nor recovered, but sits opposite me on his bed of sloth, gazing at me. He envies me the possession of the cellar key.

But of course that isn't everything. Apart from my mother and my drowned friend Richard, I have blond

Aggie and my little hunchback Boppi as angels in heaven. I have seen the houses repaired in the village and the dikes mended. If I wanted to, I could join the community council—but there are enough Camenzinds there as it is.

Recently an entirely new possibility has turned up in my life. Innkeeper Nydegger, in whose inn my father and I drank so many liters of Veltliner, Valais, and Vaud, is going downhill rapidly and no longer enjoys his trade. He complained to me about his troubles just the other day. The worst of it is, if no one from the village buys the inn, the outside brewery will, and that would be the end of it and we would be without a comfortable table. Some outside tenant would be installed who'd prefer serving beer to wine, naturally, and under whose mismanagement the good Nydegger wine-cellar would be adulterated and spoiled. I haven't stopped worrying since I found this out. I still have a little money left in my account in Basel and I wouldn't be the worst successor old Nydegger could find. The only hitch is that I would not like to become an innkeeper while my father is still alive. For not only would I be unable to keep the old man from drinking, but he would be triumphant: with all my studying and Latin, I'd have ended up as the Nimikon innkeeper. That would not do at all, and so I am marking time until my old man passes on—not impatiently, mind you, only for the sake of the cause.

After many quiet, drowsy years, Uncle Konrad is
again thirsting for adventure, and I don't like it at all.
He goes about with a finger in his mouth, his forehead
wrinkled in thought, strides around his room with quick
little steps and, when the weather is good, peers across
the lake. "I'm beginning to think he wants to build boats
again," remarked his wife, Cenzine. Indeed, Konrad
looks livelier and more daring than he has for years,
with such a sly, superior look, as if he knew exactly
what he was doing this time. But I don't believe there's
anything to it. Most likely, it is just his tired soul longing for wings to take it homeward soon. Time to put on
sails, old uncle! But once that time arrives, the people
of Nimikon will be treated to an unheard-of spectacle.
For I have decided that when Uncle Konrad's life has
ended, I myself shall say a few words at his graveside,
something unknown in these parts. I will commemo-
rate him as a blessed and beloved son of God, and
follow this edifying part with a good handful of acid
remarks for the beloved mourners, remarks they will
neither forget nor want to forgive for some time to
come. I hope my father will be around to witness the
occasion.

And in my drawer lie the beginnings of my great
work. "My Life's Work" I might call it—but that sounds
too pretentious. I'd rather not call it that, because, I
must confess, its continuation and conclusion seem

highly doubtful. Perhaps a time will come when I'll start all over again and see it through to the end. In that case, the yearning of my youth will be proved right, and I will turn out to be a poet after all.

This would mean as much, or perhaps more, to me than being a village councilor—or the builder of the stone dams. Yet it could never mean as much to me as the years of my youth that are gone but not lost, or as much as the memory of all those beloved people, from slender Rösi Girtanner to poor Boppi.

CPSIA information can be obtained
at www.ICGtesting.com
Printed in the USA
LVHW042034120123
737039LV00001B/131